The Marquis
AND THE VIXEN

The Blue Rose Regency Romances:
The Culpepper Misses, Book Two

COLLETTE CAMERON

Blue Rose Romance®
Portland, Oregon

Sweet-to-Spicy Timeless Romance®

THE MARQUIS AND THE VIXEN
The Blue Rose Regency Romances: The Culpepper Misses
Copyright © 2016 Collette Cameron
Cover Design by: Teresa Spreckelmeyer

Blue Rose Romance®
8420 N Ivanhoe # 83054
Portland, Oregon 97203

ISBN Paperback: 978-1940064673
ISBN eBook: 978-1942368182
www.collettecameron.com

Then I regret, my lord, that I must decline your offer of marriage. I'll not be married and widowed within a day's time."

"An immensely enjoyable warm-hearted and fun Regency."
~*USA Today Bestselling Author Ella Quinn*

Other Collette Cameron Books

The Honorable Rogues™
A Kiss for a Rogue
A Bride for a Rogue
A Rogue's Scandalous Wish
To Capture a Rogue's Heart
The Rogue and the Wallflower
A Rose for a Rogue

Castle Brides Series
The Viscount's Vow
Highlander's Hope
The Earl's Enticement
Heart of a Highlander (*prequel to Highlander's Hope*)

The Blue Rose Regency Romances:
The Culpepper Misses Series
The Earl and the Spinster
The Marquis and the Vixen
The Lord and the Wallflower
The Buccaneer and the Bluestocking
The Lieutenant and the Lady

Highland Highland Heather Romancing a Scot Series
Triumph and Treasure
Virtue and Valor
Heartbreak and Honor
Scandal's Splendor
Passion and Plunder
Seductive Surrender
A Yuletide Highlander

Wicked Earls' Club
Earl of Wainthorpe
Earl of Scarborough

Dedication

To Collette's Chéris

My stupendous Street Team, especially JH, AD, LE,

JG, DF, NP, DI, JB, and so many more!

Thank you! Thank you!

Xoxo

Acknowledgements

An enormous thanks to Ella Quinn for providing The Marquis and the Vixen's cover quote, to SH for your spot-on critiques, to my dedicated beta readers who catch so much that I miss after reading the same sentence a hundred times, to Teresa Spreckelmeyer for creating The Marquis and the Vixen's breathtakingly unique cover, and to ©The Beau Monde, particularly Nancy Mayor, for all of your invaluable historical expertise.

xoxo

Collette

With a determined tilt of her head, she sucked in a calming breath and returned Heath's encouraging smile.

He and Brooke preceded Blythe and her cousin, Brette, into the immense entry. Blythe's twin sisters, Blaire and Blaike, slowly wandered in wearing identical wide-eyed, stunned expressions.

Taking in the ostentatious manor, and the more flamboyant assemblage, Blythe craned her neck, catching her toe on Brooke's slipper. "Excuse me."

Perchance as boggled by the crass display of wealth, Brooke didn't respond, just slowly swung head this way and that.

Beneath the glaring candlelight of two eight-foot chandeliers, Blythe blinked again, as did her sisters and cousins—five flaxen-haired, gawping country bumpkins brought to Town.

Who could blame them?

They'd been accustomed to starkness, want, and poverty, and the grandiose entry sparkled like the Pharaoh's tomb she'd once seen in a drawing.

The urge to hike her gown to her knees and bolt to the carriage's safe and anonymous confines—like the fairytale character Cendrillon—had Blythe grasping her frothy skirt with both hands, one white-satin-slippered foot half-raised.

Whose beef-witted idea had it been to introduce the Culpeppers to society?

Heath's. Their proxy fairy godmother. He believed it might prove amusing.

To whom?

Her fan clutched in one hand—too bad it wasn't a magical wand with mythical powers—Blythe surreptitiously lifted her gown a fraction and disentangled her slipper's beaded toe from her hem again. At this rate, she'd make a spectacle of herself before she'd stepped onto the dance floor, the singular thing she hadn't dreaded. Musically inclined her whole life, the prospect of dancing didn't worry her. *Much.*

Their ensemble had drawn considerable attention already, some speculation less than affable from the barbed stares and pouting moues slung their way, and tonight's introduction to *la beau monde* was important to Brooke's and the other girls' success.

None of the Culpeppers had relished visiting London, but these past weeks had changed everyone's minds, excluding Blythe's. The streets boasted refuse and manure, and the city stank worse than the dairy barns during summer's peak temperatures. Beggars and orphans abounded, as did women of loose virtue. The stark contrast between the opulent display currently surrounding her and the hollow-eyed, raggarbed street urchins she'd seen on the drive here grated.

Grossly unfair, the patent disparity.

Perhaps enduring years of hunger and lack had embittered her toward the affluent more than she'd realized.

"Look at the cherubs and nymphs." Her voice low and lilting with amused embarrassment, Brette elbowed Blythe. "They're everywhere and completely naked."

They were indeed.

As the majordomo announced their troupe in an onerous monotone, Blythe answered the smile of a striking man, who dipped his curly, sun-kissed head at her. Broad-shouldered, with a sculpted face, and attired in the height of fashion, he was quite the handsomest man she'd ever seen.

Merriment lit his features, and his smile blossomed into a satisfied grin. His fawn-colored gaze lazily traveled from her insignificant bosoms to her toes then made the reverse journey to once again hover on her breasts before boldly meeting her eyes. His pleated at the corners again, a testament to a man accustomed to smiling habitually.

Her stomach reacted most peculiarly, all floppy and churning.

And her breasts?

Why, under his appreciative regard, the dratted insignificant things swelled and pebbled proudly. Quite forward of them, given their unimpressive size. Warmth skidded up the angles of her cheeks, and she averted her gaze.

Hound's teeth.

First time she'd ever blushed or had her bosoms betray her. Next thing she knew, the perky pair would scramble from her bodice's lace edge and wave a jaunty hello.

Her cousin edged nearer and splayed her fan, concealing their lower faces. She bobbed her fair head to indicate the ballroom entrance where a crowd spilled forth, perusing and prattling about the newcomers. "Look, Blythe. The statues on either side of those double doors are too."

"Are what?" What was Brette yammering about? Oh. Naked. The statues of Greek gods were naked as a needle. "Must be why those silly girls are giggling and pointing."

Raised on a farm, Blaike smirked and Blaire grinned, their pansy-blue eyes twinkling. The male anatomy didn't intrigue them quite as singularly as it obviously did the sheltered society misses. Nonetheless, the statues' manly endowments left nothing to the imagination.

Well, one remained endowed.

The other's male bits had snapped off in a debutante's hand, causing another round of frenetic tittering. From the way their scolding hostess descended upon the women, Blythe would have bet her pendant the god had lost his penis to curious groping before.

"Thought you might need a hand, Ravensdale." A mocking male addressed Heath from over Blythe's right shoulder.

Good God.

Blythe stiffened, refusing to look behind her.

The rumbling baritone could belong to only one man. The insufferable Marquis of Leventhorpe.

Perfectly horrid.

Her first foray into High Society, and he attended the same gathering, his presence as welcome as a crotchety, old tabby cat. He'd rubbed her wrong, and they'd crossed words, ever since meeting at Esherton Green, her childhood home. A more arrogant, difficult ... humorless ... stubborn person than Lord Leventhorpe didn't strut the Earth.

His scent, crisp linen mixed with sandalwood, enveloped her, warning her he'd drawn nearer. Too near. His breath tickled her ear as he mumbled almost inaudibly, "Your mouth was hanging open like a pelican's. Again."

She pressed her lips together and steadfastly disregarded the distracting jolt his closeness and warm breath caused. He'd startled her. Nothing else.

What's a blasted pelican?

Something with a vast mouth, no doubt, but dancing naked atop hot coals was preferable to asking the behemoth to explain.

"What a rag-mannered boor you are to mention it, my lord." Speaking under her breath and from the side of her mouth, she commanded her lips to curve congenially while examining her family and mentally cursing him to Hades.

For once, no one noticed their verbal sparring.

Looming several inches above her, Lord Leventhorpe's chest—a thick, wide wall of virile maleness—blocked her view. Tempted to shift away, she forced her feet to stay planted. He was the largest man she'd ever met, and as one of Heath's closest friends, she must learn to tolerate Lord Leventhorpe's intimidating presence. Surely sainthood and a seat at the Lord's Table awaited her if she managed the Herculean task.

The auburn-haired devil enjoyed provoking her, and like a nincompoop, she regularly succumbed to his goading. She normally possessed a level head, and that he should be the person to have her at sixes and sevens, exasperated her.

A growl of frustration formed in her throat, and she clenched her teeth and hands.

"Ravensdale, you have your hands full." Leventhorpe skirted her, giving a cynical twist of his shapely lips as he passed. "I would deem it the ultimate privilege to assist you with these exquisite ladies."

She didn't believe his sycophantic posturing for an instant. At Esherton, when he'd accused the Culpeppers of abducting Heath, she'd seen the real Lord Leventhorpe, and this fawning deference concealed a stone-hearted, grim-tempered cawker.

His penetrating gaze—as heated and blue as a cloudless noonday sky in August—probed hers as if he strove to read her mind and emotions. Most disconcerting, and none of his blasted business. Maddening how he scrambled her thoughts and agitated feelings she couldn't decipher.

A spurt of amusement lit his eyes, and she narrowed hers.

Stop staring, you oversized, handsome baboon.

Immediately, Lord Leventhorpe's expression became shuttered and inscrutable. He rubbed the side of his nose and canvassed the entry before offering an enigmatic half-smile. "If you need help escorting the ladies, Hawksworth and I would be honored to assist."

"Reverend Hawksworth is here too?" Blythe peered over her shoulder.

Yes, indeed. Grinning, Reverend Hawksworth wended his way through the throng.

Charming, witty, and the perfect gentleman, he rivaled the fair god who'd smiled at her earlier. She slanted Lord Leventhorpe a contemplative glance. How could such two startlingly dissimilar men—one angelic and one demonic—be Heath's closest friends?

Brette perked up, her cheeks pinkening and eyes sparkling when the cleric joined them. At Esherton Green, Blythe had suspected her cousin's interest in Reverend Hawksworth, and Brette's reaction tonight confirmed it.

Chuckling, he cut his jungle-eyed gaze to the gawkers surging from the ballroom. "I do believe a near insurrection is at hand. Arriving with five incomparables is hardly fair play, Raven. I expect histrionics, swooning, and apoplexy in record numbers this evening. Perchance a bit of fervent, and not altogether hallowed, petitioning of the Almighty as well."

Nodding at something the butler said, Heath grinned. "Ah, I never intended fair play. I would wager appeared brown from a distance.

He flashed a rakish smile, revealing well-tended teeth.

Splendid. She couldn't abide poor hygiene.

"Hawksworth, I beg you. Introduce me to these charming ladies, so I might claim a dance with each." Though the Adonis included Brette in his appeal, his gaze never left Blythe, and the curving of his lips caused another unfamiliar jolt.

The reverend shook his head. "Too late, Burlington. I've already requested sets and the supper dance with Miss Brette." He slightly raised the arm her fingers lay upon. "And Ravensdale ought to make the introductions, not me."

Burlington—was he a mister? A Lord? Something else?—wrinkled his forehead in mock horror. "Troublesome etiquette rules." His brandy-tinted gaze sought Blythe's. "If Ravensdale agrees, would you favor me with the supper dance?"

A trifle forward, but ...

"I would like that." No feigning diffidence. He was an attractive man, and he'd captured her interest in the entry, something unanticipated, truth to tell. "I must confess, I don't claim a substantial appetite."

For years, the Culpeppers had survived on insufficient food, and although they had plenty to eat now, she couldn't manage generous portions. Given her height, she doubted she'd ever possess an enticingly rounded figure like the young ladies occupying the bench farther along. The figures of the older women with them had evolved into rotundness—not something Blythe worried about.

Once the rest of their group made it to the bench—Leventhorpe, a dark, menacing deity dwarfing everyone, his keen, raptor gaze combing the ballroom—Heath made quick work of the introductions.

Blythe's admirer was Mr. Courtland Burlington, the second son of the Earl of Lauderdale. No title, therefore no worries about a lowly gentlewoman aiming her sights too high.

Not that she'd set her cap for Mr. Burlington. Much too soon for that. This was her first assembly, after all. Nonetheless, he presented quite a dashing figure and, given the envious looks regularly flitting in his direction, much sought after by females.

"I'm delighted to make your acquaintance, Miss Culpepper." Mr. Burlington lifted her hand as he bowed, kissing the air above her fingers. A stickler for propriety or affecting courtly conduct? Would he mind awfully that she found decorum about as useful as a well-gnawed chicken bone?

Culpepper recognized a poltroon when she met one. Or possibly, it was Tristan who aroused her suspicion. Given their instant, mutual animosity, the latter seemed more likely, especially since he had broken Sheridan Gainsborough's nose when Gainsborough interfered with Ravensdale's wedding.

"Yes, I did. And no. I don't." Tristan refused to be baited, and her slightly rouged lips thinned a fraction, a mysterious glint shadowing her eyes. At least he assumed her mouth rouged. Too dewy and rosy to be natural, surely, unless she'd dined upon berries recently.

What kind?

A taste of her delicious mouth, made for hungry kisses and sensual smiles, would answer the question. A blast of sensation straight to his groin strangled his carnal musings.

What the hell is wrong with me, lusting after a woman who clearly loathes me?

Fiddling with her fan, she took Phillips's measure, toe to top before scooting Tristan a covert peek. Good manners prohibited her asking the how and why of his corking Phillips. Nonetheless, her expressive eyes fairly shouted for an answer.

How would she respond if he told her?

Well, you see, Miss Culpepper, it started with a

pox-ridden whore, and Hawksworth, the reluctant vicar.

"Phillips, when did you return to England?" Ravensdale's question broke the weighty silence and wrenched Tristan abruptly back to the bustling ballroom.

Flouting propriety and drumming his fingertips along the bench, Ravensdale made no effort to introduce Phillips to the ladies. Brilliant strategy upon Raven's part. Without an introduction, Phillips couldn't address the women directly. When he'd married Brooke, Ravensdale had vowed to protect the Culpepper ladies, and his decorum breach proved his seriousness.

Phillips hauled his appreciative gaze from the women, pique sharpening his angular face. "A month ago. And I'm glad I did, else I would have missed this," he gestured to the exquisite blondes, his hint as brazen as a skirtless harlot, "delightful spectacle."

Still not getting an introduction, you bugger.

Phillips offered his usual suave smile.

No Culpepper responded with anything more enthusiastic than a placid gaze. Not even the twins— the youngest, most impressionable of the lot.

Uncanny how two people could look exactly alike. Dressed in identical gowns except for the color, he had no idea who was Blaire and who was Blaike. How old were they again? Scratching his eyebrow, he wracked his brain. Had anyone ever told him? How old was Blythe, for that matter?

She observed Phillips, a marginal pucker between her winged brows.

As if sensing Tristan's scrutiny, Blythe swiftly schooled her features into blandness once more while unfurling her fan. However, she couldn't conceal the spark glinting in her iris eyes. A sapphire-violet fire, waiting to be fanned into flames, smoldered below her composed surface. He'd seen the firestorm more than once—truthfully, he'd caused a conflagration or two— and found her temper invigorating.

How perverse.

A knowing glance passed between Lady Ravensdale and Brette before their nonchalant gazes returned to Phillips as well.

Yes, by God. All five were on to old Phillips and his reptilian wiles.

Good thing too.

He'd fathered more than one by-blow, and suggestions had circulated for years that the serving wenches hadn't willingly engaged in the dalliances. No doubt his female servants lamented his return to London. *Le beau monde* had been blessed with his absence for two—or was it three?—years while the cull toured the continent before journeying to India. At least that was the drivel his sire, the viscount, spread about Town.

Tristan didn't believe a syllable, especially after a highborn young woman became scarce and later hastily married an elderly sot before giving birth to a daughter a mere four months after the nuptials. Tattle had it, Phillips had ravished her.

The woman's father, the Duke of Coventry, had threated to call Phillips out, hence the cur's abrupt departure from England. Awfully convenient, Coventry's dying recently, paving the way for Phillips to scuttle home and muck about in the dank dens he favored. Rumors had circulated that Phillips's father, the doting and blind-to-his-son's-faults Viscount Rotherton, had greased more than one fist to assure his son escaped justice.

Phillips resembled an enormous cockroach—Tristan's nostrils quivered—right down to the sour smell that copious quantities of cologne failed to completely conceal.

"Memories are peculiar things, aren't they, Whitehouse? They're quite dependent upon the perceptions of the person recollecting." Reverend Hawksworth lifted a short, blond hair from his forearm, inclining his head toward Phillips.

Perturbed, Phillips pressed his lips into a pout, his regard of the Culpeppers bordering upon lascivious.

"I seem to recall that after insulting Leventhorpe, Phillips took the first swing." Hand straddling his hip, Hawk regarded Whitehouse.

"Aye, that's my memory as well. What say you, Drake?" Dislike deepened the lines framing the captain's mouth and feathering the corners of his eyes. He flexed his fingers near his waist as if instinctively reaching for a cutlass.

Hands clasped behind his back, Drake nodded, his eyes flinty. "Indeed. That's exactly how I remember it too."

"You were ape-drunk that night, Hawksworth. How could *you* remember anything?" Phillips's mouth slid into a sideways sneer as he bared his craven talons. "Isn't drunkenness one of the sins you preach against?"

Miss Brette's eyes rounded, and her mouth parted as she and the Culpeppers, plus Lady Ravensdale, swung their attention to Hawksworth's flushed face.

Had Phillips forgotten Hawk's pugilist skills? Even a man of God possessed limited patience. From his sharply drawn brows and balled fists, Hawksworth might be near his snapping point.

How would Phillips like his nose shattered again? Or mayhap his jaw this go round? Hawk could easily do either.

"Stubble it, Phillips." Tristan's warning met with an unrepentant, cocky grin.

The one time Hawk had gotten pished, and for a bloody good reason too, and Phillips, the colossal arse, had to humiliate him for it. Typical.

Blythe speared Phillips a scorching glower, muttering something inaudible beneath her breath and behind her fan which sounded suspiciously like cod's head or codpiece.

Knowing her, probably the latter. Tristan rather appreciated the comparison.

"Gentlemen, this discussion is wholly inappropriate, especially with young ladies present." Lady Ravensdale stood and motioned to the younger women, succinctly ending the unpleasantness. "I'll thank you to cease or continue it elsewhere. Besides, I should like to dance with my husband since I haven't had the opportunity. Blythe, would you please act as chaperone until I return?"

"Of course." Blythe offered Mr. Burlington a penitent smile, and annoyance poked Tristan's ribs. Hard. She'd never been half as accommodating or agreeable to him.

What did he care?

A more provoking, outspoken virago he'd never had the ill-fortune to meet. His embittered mother notwithstanding, God rest her tormented soul.

Truthfully, being the primary beneficiary of Blythe's dislike grated.

In response to Burlington's proprietary smile, she curved her lips, her cheeks acquiring the same flushed glow as her mouth.

Perhaps she wasn't that perceptive after all. True, Burlington was a pleasant enough fellow, but as many young blades were wont to do, he generally treated women as passing amusements, something to trifle with and conquer until another caught his fancy. Nevertheless, women had tamed rakehells far worse than him.

Tristan gave a mental shrug. No concern of his.

He'd been asked to help a friend, and that was the only reason he'd accepted the Kattenbys' invitation tonight. Suppressing a yawn, he perused the ballroom, still humming about the Culpeppers.

Bloody insane. That's what Raven is.

One or two beauties might have been manageable, but five? Humor jerked the corners of Tristan's mouth. His friend would rue the day he'd ever entertained this hair-brained notion. Wouldn't surprise him if Raven wound up bald as a billiard by Season's end, and he had nice hair too.

Set the *le beau monde* upon its arse, indeed.

"I shall save the next set for you, Mr. Burlington." The beatific smile Blythe bestowed upon Burlington squeezed Tristan's lungs.

Damnation. And double damn that he'd noticed.

"That won't be necessary, Blythe. You may dance this set." Though Ravensdale's lips slanted, no humor glinted in the astute gaze he raked over Phillips. "Whitehouse and Drake, I would appreciate you escorting a twin onto the dance floor, and I've already given Hawk permission to dance with Miss Brette."

Well done. Tristan indulged in a gloating grin.

Ravensdale had snuffed Phillips's intent to beg an introduction and a dance with one of the sisters or cousins faster than a pinched candlewick. He wouldn't be adding one of their number to his list of conquests.

"I would beg you save me the supper dance then, Miss Culpepper, since I won't have the pleasure of a dancing this set." Tristan couldn't resist goading Phillips, knowing full well Ravensdale would accept Tristan's request as speedily as he'd spurned Phillips's.

Ravensdale's stunned expression was reflected in the other astounded gazes whipping to Tristan.

Hell.

Ignoring the impulse would have been wiser except he'd agreed to dance with each Culpepper. Damn awkward, this doing the pretty balderdash. No more favors for friends. Tristan suspected Ravensdale intended to utilize him, and perhaps poor Hawk, as surrogates to help chaperone and manage the goddesses the entire season.

Not bloody well likely. Tristan truly couldn't abide crowds for extended periods. An hour at most, and he made for the exit.

A disgusting memory assailed him, rendering him mute and immobile for a moment. Swallowing a surge of nausea, he shook his head to dispel the buzzing in his ears and the sudden onslaught of dizziness.

What had they been discussing?

The supper dance.

Had Blythe responded? "Miss Culpepper?"

What else could he say? He hadn't a clue whether she had answered.

Her lively gaze assessing, Blythe slanted her head the merest bit, the amber gems entwined in her curls winking under the chandelier's radiance. "I'm sorry, Lord Leventhorpe, I already promised the supper dance to Mr. Burlington."

"Perhaps a waltz later, then." Tristan flexed his fingers against the desire to wipe the delighted smile from Burlington's face.

Give over, Trist. You'd have the same smirk on your face if she'd said yes to you.

He would've?

The awareness gave him pause.

He would.

Only because it withered his ballocks to have coxcombs like Burlington best him.

"Blythe." Subtle censure tinted Lady Ravensdale's tone. "You've other unclaimed dances."

Tristan almost stuck a finger in his ear and wiggled it to make sure he'd heard correctly. Had she encouraged her cousin to dance with him? Some turnabout there.

"I shall save you the last waltz, Lord Leventhorpe." A corpse displayed more genuine enthusiasm upon being laid in a coffin. Blythe looped her hand through Burlington's elbow and glided away, laughing at something he murmured to her. She'd never appeared more vivacious or beautiful.

Giving Phillips a contemptuous glare—and hopefully a parson's curse damning him to purgatory—Hawksworth offered Miss Brette his arm, and they set out after the others.

A bevy of whispers behind fans and gloved hands trailed the Culpeppers' progress. Gentlemen peered with brazen interest through their quizzing glasses, while ill-disguised envy pinched many ladies' features. A goodly number of friendly smiles greeted them too.

Yes, Raven had stirred a beehive, and when bees are riled, someone is sure to get stung.

Tristan searched for a servant. After that exchange he welcomed a glass of punch. No. He really wanted a finger or two of whisky, but he was a quarter way to bosky already.

"Seems like you and I have been found wanting, Leventhorpe." Phillips glared after the departing couples.

First sting went to Phillips. That bounder could expect many more sharp pricks from Raven and the Culpeppers.

"Don't include me in your company. I spent several days as a guest of the Culpeppers at their country estate." Vast exaggeration there. He'd arrived at Esherton Green looking for Ravensdale and had refused to leave without his friend. And calling their malodorous dairy farm and ramshackle house an estate was equivalent to calling the Prince Regent a Devil's Acre beggar.

"Awful uppity for country wenches." Phillips scratched his prominent chin. "Though I wouldn't mind sampling their charms. I admit a penchant for blondes. That one in yellow is a prime article and seems the most spirited. I've found that trait commonly carries into bedding the gel."

A fury-induced haze momentarily stole Tristan's tongue.

"Makes for a delicious shagging." His voice deepened by lust, Phillips licked his lips. "Especially if they resist."

Would the House of Lords bring charges against Tristan if he disposed of Phillips once and for all? Probably. Even if they celebrated the cur's demise with fireworks and Champagne afterward. Subduing his wrath, he drew his spine upright, fully aware his immense size daunted shorter men.

He scowled down at Phillips. "Unless you want me to break your nose again, I suggest you take your leave. *Now.* And stay away from the Culpeppers—"

"Tristan, dearest." His cousin's singsong voice beset him.

He speared a gaze heavenward, begging God for patience as she, no doubt prompted by her domineering companion, Rosemary Sanford, glided his way. He'd exhausted his reserves of forbearance by not pummeling Phillips and had scant left to cushion his terse response to Francine.

"You were saying, Leventhorpe?" His lips skewed

mockingly, Phillips folded his arms.

Francine seized Tristan's forearm. "Tristan, I told Rosemary you would dance with her this evening since you rudely left the last ball without doing as you'd promised."

He hadn't promised.

Francine had pleaded with him to dance with her friend, and he'd said he'd consider it. He'd done so, contemplating the notion for a lengthy two seconds before deciding he'd prefer to go home and cut his already groomed toenails.

Why Francine kowtowed to the likes of Rosemary Sanford, he couldn't imagine. Though irrefutably beautiful, Miss Sanford was an inconsiderate friend, and he'd bet Bristledale Court and his mother's many glittery baubles that she had manipulated Francine to get to him.

That woman hunted for a title this Season, or he was a twiddle poop.

At eight and twenty, his poor, spinster cousin desperately strove for acceptance and regularly made a cake of herself to please her scheming friend.

That nettled more than Miss Sanford's designs on the marquisate.

"Since Leventhorpe is escorting Miss Sanford, may I request the next set, Miss Simmons?" Phillips extended his arm, challenging Tristan to say no.

Phillips clearly baited Tristan, and as tempted as he was to tell Francine not to, she probably hadn't enjoyed more than a dance or two this evening. Most assemblies, she didn't dance except with Tristan. She'd gaze longingly at laughing couples while huddled with the other plain wallflowers.

If she could abide Phillips's sweet and sour odor for the dance's duration, Tristan wouldn't begrudge her a few moments of happiness.

Francine colored, her cheeks two candy-apple red blotches, and grasped Phillips's elbow a mite too exuberantly. "I'd be delighted, Mr. Phillips."

Smiling coquettishly, Miss Sanford blinked her big, brown calf-eyes at him. "You wouldn't snub me in full view of the Kattenbys' guests, would you, my lord?

The wise woman recognizes and disdains
the schemes of pretentious social climbers.
~Dignity and Decorum—The Genteel Lady's
Guide to Practical Living

3

After wandering down a corridor, Blythe slowly ambled to a stop.

This wasn't right. Nothing seemed the least familiar.

Botheration.

She searched the passageway behind her. After leaving the lady's retiring room, she'd apparently taken a wrong corridor. Or two. She had best retrace her steps before she found herself completely turned round.

She possessed a dismal sense of direction. If she ever found herself in the heart of London without an escort, she would wander about in circles for a month. Then again, it might take them that long to find her in this astonishingly vast and complex house.

The next dance belonged to Lord Leventhorpe. She smiled, a trifle impishly. Perhaps her conscience had deliberately misguided her to avoid what was sure to be a trying half an hour. She'd be obligated to bear his touch and converse with him the whole while.

Considering their longest prior communication hadn't been above five minutes, they might scratch one another's eyes out before the music ended. Lifting her skirt to enable her to walk quicker, she grinned. Mayhap she ought to remove her gloves. Her nails were longer. He, on the other hand, was much taller.

Truthfully, her preoccupation leading to her becoming lost could be blamed on pleasurable musings about Mr. Burlington.

Her cotillion with him had been lovely. An excellent dancer, he possessed a ready wit and a readier smile. More importantly, he made her comfortable. They'd conversed and laughed easily, and when their dance ended, Blythe admitted she'd been startled and not a little disappointed. She'd never expected to meet a gentleman of his caliber this early on, and he'd quite assailed her logic and senses.

Usually a pragmatic woman, her woolgathering was as foreign and distasteful as those strange fishy-smelling black beads their hostess had served at a dinner party three nights ago.

Blythe had taken a spin around the ballroom with several distinguished gentlemen. And she'd refused an equal number of disappointed beaux's requests, because she'd already promised the remainder to others. Mr. Burlington's had been the most enjoyable by far.

In his company, she forgot the crowd and hubbub, and she happily anticipated the supper dance and dining with him. Her next partner didn't rouse the same cheery expectation.

Whatever had possessed Lord Leventhorpe to ask for a dance? And a waltz, no less.

More importantly, whyever had she agreed?

He'd stirred her sympathy, she grudgingly admitted. That knowledge practically sent her into an apoplexy. A shiver raised her flesh, and she briskly rubbed her arms above her elbow-length gloves. Gads, just thinking about Lord Leventhorpe agitated her.

Two corridors intersected, and she paused to collect her bearings.

Right or left?

Ah, the marble-topped mahogany table with the heinous vase she'd seen before.

Now I remember.

Whisking along, her slippers silent upon the

burgundy Aubusson runner, Blythe passed the table. Another two turns, and she'd be at the landing. She held her breath, straining to hear the music as she marched along.

A quadrille. Not too late after all, devil it.

Lord Leventhorpe would have his troublesome waltz. If she found her way downstairs again.

When she'd refused him the supper dance, she'd glimpsed something startling in the depths of his eyes. So staggering, in truth, that she'd almost gone onto tiptoe and pulled his head down to examine their blue depths closer.

Vulnerability was the last emotion she'd ever expected to see. *Ever.* He hid it well, which piqued her curiosity. What caused a man as outwardly frosty as a winter gale to disguise shyness?

Blythe loved a riddle, and Leventhorpe, it seemed, was more than he presented. "Now to uncover why." His discomfiture shadowed eyes floated before her, and she quirked her lips. "He's an enigma, to be sure."

Head bowed, she toyed with her pendant, deep in reverie as she approached a black-velvet-curtained alcove. At the corner, she bumped into a man. Smelling of rosewater and something else, a peculiar tangy scent—stale sweat, perchance?—he steadied her with surprisingly strong arms, given their wiriness.

Drat.

Mr. Phillips, another inscrutable man. In a crafty, scheming fashion rather than a mysterious, intriguing one. "Do you usually wander corridors talking to yourself?" His languid gaze slithered over her. "An unwise habit for a beauty such as yourself."

"Talking to myself is unwise?" Blythe raised a dubious brow. His lewd implication hadn't escaped her, but she wouldn't give him the satisfaction of acknowledging his crassness.

"No, I meant—" Mr. Phillips smiled and loosened his grip, though he didn't release her. "It's of no import. I believe you may have crushed my quizzing glass."

"I beg your pardon." Barely subduing the urge to recoil and hurry to the retiring room to scrub her arms where his cold, damp fingers touched her, Blythe disengaged herself and stepped backward. She hadn't hit him hard enough to break anything. "I'll replace the piece if it's damaged."

He would have to prove it first. Doubtful he owned a quizzing glass, and if he had one in his possession tonight, he'd tucked it safely away.

The lovely woman she'd seen on the other bench earlier emerged from the alcove, a syrupy smile bending her mouth as the curtain fell into place.

Hmm, interesting. Had he come from there too? Why the need for the lowered curtain?

A *tête-à-tête*?

Swathed in haughtiness, the woman swept to Mr. Phillips's side. "How clumsy of you, though to be expected from a clodpoll newly introduced to Polite Society."

Mayhap she'd like to see what else clodpolls were capable of. How much did she value her hair? Blythe could sheer a sheep in fifteen minutes. She would have those gorgeous coffee-colored locks off in ten seconds.

Much as she would've liked to give the chit a verbal set down, the music below had ceased.

She must hurry, or she would miss the waltz with his lordship. A minute ago, she'd been half-wishing that very thing, and now she was quite desperate to make sure she didn't. Mimicking the woman's lofty mien, Blythe lifted her chin and examined the passage beyond them. "As we've not been introduced, I find it presumptuous to assume you know anything about me."

"Everyone here tonight knows *who* the Culpepper interlopers are." The brunette's retort rang harsh and venom-laced.

They did? How peculiar. Had Society nothing better to occupy their consideration? That was what came of being idle and wealthy. And bitchy.

"Miss Sanford, please allow me the honor of making the introductions." Mr. Phillips offered a ghost of a bow. "Rosemary Sanford, may I present...?" He peered expectantly at Blythe, his lips edging upward into what he, no doubt, considered a charming smile. He resembled an overly sleek, grinning Cheshire cat. "I'm afraid I don't know your given name, Miss Culpepper."

And it's going to stay that way. I'm not completely ignorant of social graces.

"I believe it's proper to wait to be introduced, is it not? And that same decorum prohibits me from speaking further to you." She inclined her head. "If you'll excuse me, I've promised Lord Leventhorpe the next dance."

The rude, inarticulate sound Miss Sanford released could only be described as a hiss of displeasure. Eyes narrowed to wrathful slits, she stared down her nose at Blythe, or tried to. Rather awkward and comical when Blythe stood several inches taller.

"*You're* dancing a waltz with the marquis?" Miss Sanford's mouth curled into a full sneer.

"Yes. He's a *very close* family friend." Not quite the truth, but the jealous chit needn't know that. Besides, Miss Sanford had stood up with his lordship already. Blythe had seen her pressing into him, a seductress's smile slanting her flawless mouth. "I believe I spotted you dancing with him earlier? Why, did he not request a waltz with you also? How utterly disappointed you must be."

Truly wicked of Blythe to taunt, but Miss Sanford rose to the bait readily.

Another disgruntled sound echoed in her throat, and Miss Sanford lifted her fan threateningly.

Did she think to dictate who Lord Leventhorpe danced with? If they were more than mere acquaintances, her vexation might have merit, but on her first night amongst the upper crust, Blythe had no idea if Miss Sanford was a particular favorite of Lord Leventhorpe's. The chit certainly showed possessive tendencies and a dismal temper too.

Lord Leventhorpe hadn't seemed particularly enthralled with her company, but given his skill at concealing his emotions, his lack of exuberance didn't reveal much.

Francine Simmons emerged from the retiring room, a confused sulk marring her forehead. "There you are, Rosemary. I thought you were still inside. You left without telling me? I was waiting in the adjoining chamber as you asked me to. Did I misunderstand?"

"I needed to speak with Mr. Phillips, and I don't have to tell you my every movement, Francine. I declare, you are positively suffocating at times. I don't know how I abide you." With that snide comment, Miss Sanford gripped Mr. Phillips's arm and sallied forth, hauling him toward the stairs.

Toss pots.

He glanced behind him, giving Blythe another disturbing smile. Something queer about that man. Something uncanny—almost eerie or treacherous—in his eyes. She'd hate to bump into him alone in a secluded spot. Why, even now, with other women present, her skin tried to scamper off her bones and cower in the alcove's dark corner.

A sniffle drew her attention to the dejected woman hunched beside her.

"I don't know why I tolerate her." Miss Simmons rubbed her red-rimmed eyes, worsening their appearance. "On a charitable day she's selfish and inconsiderate ... and entirely thoughtless."

"I'm sorry." Oh, to be able to shave that snotty-nosed miss's head bare as a hog's bristly behind. "Is there anything I can do to help?"

"No. I'm just overwrought. I shall be fine in a moment or two." Miss Simmons shook her head and produced a despairing little laugh. "I have fragile nerves, Rosemary says."

Hmm, with that creature for a friend, the Lord himself would require a calming draught. An immense one.

"I'm Blythe Culpepper." Offering a sunny smile, Blythe touched Miss Simmons's elbow. So much for propriety. Blythe fished her handkerchief from her bodice. "Here. Dry your eyes, and I shall walk to the ballroom with you. Who are you here with?"

Miss Simmons wiped her face then blew her nose. "I came with Rosemary, her mother, and grandmother. I live alone, you see. Well, I have a small staff. My parents are dead, and Tristan, that is, Lord Leventhorpe, is my only living relation. We're second cousins." Melancholy tinged her voice. "Rosemary permits me to accompany her to social gatherings as long as I do as she bids."

I'll bet she does.

She patted another tear leaking from the corner of her eye.

"You live alone? Why don't you live with Lord Leventhorpe?" How could he permit this obviously lonely woman to reside by herself?'

"Oh, Tristan has offered, many times, but I want my independence. Mama and Papa left me enough to be comfortable if I economize, and if I lived in the country with him— Oh, dear. I oughtn't to have shared that. Utterly gauche." Her face blooming with color, she hunched a shoulder. "I hold a trifling hope that I might meet a gentleman who would take me to wife. Silly, I know."

Pained rejection reduced her voice to a whisper with her last words, and Blythe's heart wrenched. Mere weeks ago, her circumstances had been desperate and seemingly impossible, until Heath had rescued them. Who would rescue Francine?

Lord Leventhorpe?

Perhaps a word in his ear was in order, though he didn't seem the sort to readily take suggestions. If intervening helped this pitiable woman, the effort was worth annoying his lordship.

"A lovely woman such as yourself, Miss Simmons, should continue to harbor that wonderful dream."

"Thank you. You are most kind." At Blythe's compliment, Miss Simmons's mouth formed a surprised O and color dashed her face again. "Rosemary said beautiful women like you ..." Cheeks deepening to crimson, she cast her gaze to the floor. "Never mind. I'm sure she is mistaken."

Blythe had a pretty fair notion what Miss Sanford had told Miss Simmons.

Miss Simmons's possessed a good complexion, her gray-blue eyes held keen intelligence, and her hair shimmered with the same umber shades as Lord Leventhorpe's. If she wore the right colors and styles—not like the drab oatmeal-colored sack she had on—arranged her striking hair differently, and added the faintest touch of cosmetics, she would be quite attractive. Her self-confidence was an entirely other matter.

Perhaps Blythe and the other Culpeppers might assist in that regard. And keeping Miss Simmons away from that self-serving Sanford banshee seemed the obvious place to start.

The prelude's first few notes drifted up from below, and Blythe quickened her pace. During the dance would be the perfect time to broach the subject of his lordship's cousin.

"Lord Leventhorpe doesn't stay with you when he comes to town?" Probably had a house. Bachelors didn't like the restrictions of living with female relatives. At least her nefarious cousin Sheridan never had. Thank God the Chancery Court had appointed Heath their guardian, ridding the Culpeppers of ever having to deal with Sheridan again.

"No, Tristan has lodgings at White's. He quite loathes London and never stays at his house on

Mayfair. I'm not sure he even maintains staff there. He only ventures to Town for important Parliamentary matters." Brushing a tendril away from her eye, Miss Simmons gave a sad smile. "You needn't pity me. I don't mind being alone. I have my charitable meetings and Church. And every now and again, I receive an invitation to call."

When was the last time anyone had listened to the poor dear? Blythe smiled tolerantly as Miss Simmons prattled on, oblivious to the pair of ladies approaching from the other direction. Stepping to the side, Blythe waited for them to pass and answered their friendly smiles with her own.

"And I enjoy reading. Have you been to The Temple of the Muses, Miss Culpepper? Such a wonderful bookshop. Oh, and I quite adore riding. Tristan takes me two or three times a week when he's here. He is a dear underneath his aloof manner. His mother was dotty, you see, and his father ..." Cutting Blythe a hesitant, sidelong glance, she chewed her lower lip indecisively.

"His father?"

Miss Simmons was a store of useful information. It gushed from her like milk from a cow's full teat. There was much more to the reserved marquis then Blythe had imagined. Not that she'd imagined anything about him, of course, other than uncharitable thoughts at Esherton Green when she'd pondered if he'd docked his devil's tail, how often he filed the horns his hair concealed, and how he managed to shove his cloven hooves into boots.

Miss Simmons exhaled a hefty breath and scooted closer. "The former Lord Leventhorpe was a lecherous, depraved scoundrel." Her voice soft and low, she nervously peered around. "Or so I've heard whispered. No one tells a lady anything directly, for fear of our tender sensibilities—most irritating and utterly ridiculous—but for years I've overheard snatches about his deplorable behavior."

Splendid. Miss Simmons had a fiery streak buried in her. Though how could she not when she shared Leventhorpe's blood?

Blythe looped her hand through Miss Simmons's crooked elbow. "I have two sisters, and we have lived with our two cousins since I was eight. The five of us get along famously, but sometimes I crave time alone."

"Miss Culpepper, would you ...?" Miss Simmons screwed up her courage and blurted, "Would you come for tea? Your sisters and cousins, too?"

Evidently accustomed to rejection, her eyes round and anxious, she fiddled with the folds of her fan.

Blythe grinned and nodded. "If you agree to call

me Blythe."

"And you must call me Francine." They reached the staircase's bottom. "I was named after Tristan's mother."

Arm in arm, they entered the ballroom, and coppery hair, a head taller than the rest of the guests, snagged her attention. Arms crossed and his countenance one of polite boredom, Lord Leventhorpe leaned a shoulder against an arched windowsill and perused the room. From the black of his cutaway coat and breeches, to the gold and burgundy of his waistcoat, he blended with the decor.

His languid gaze roved the entrance, and he straightened upon spying her.

An amiable smile brightened his face, his attention dipping to Francine before swooping back to Blythe. His lips bent more as he strode in their direction, moving with the lithe, natural grace of an athlete, his long legs rapidly covering the distance.

Had he watched for her?

Upon reaching them, he executed an exaggerated courtier's bow, and Francine giggled.

Even Blythe's lips curved at his silliness. She'd not have believed him capable of the overplayed gallantry.

"Trist, you're uncommonly chipper." Francine

touched his arm, peering at him hopefully "Did you enjoy your dance with Rosemary, then?"

Blythe quashed her irritation. It would take time to wean Francine from her dependency upon Miss Sanford's self-serving approval.

"It was unremarkable." Though he answered Francine, his attention remained upon Blythe.

Francine's face fell, her earlier buoyancy evaporating. "Oh. I'd hoped ... Never mind."

He chucked her chin. "But, my dear, I saved the supper dance for you. Now tell me. What have you two ladies been up to?"

"You did? The supper dance, truly?" Francine beamed once more. "Blythe ... I mean Miss Culpepper, has been most kind and graciously consented to come for tea."

Goodness. Miss Simmons's emotions vacillated hot and cold.

Lord Leventhorpe's chestnut brows shot skyward. "Indeed. Might I join you?"

Francine's jaw slackened, and she blinked, rather like a confused owl. "Of course. Why, I believe I shall ask the Culpeppers to call. And Reverend Hawksworth. He's always kind. Oh, and the Wimpletons, of course." She glanced around. "I must find something to write on. Please excuse me." She hustled off, a plump brown wren, decidedly cheerier than she had been upstairs.

"What have you done to my cousin?" Extending his elbow, Lord Leventhorpe stared after her retreating form. "I don't recall when I've seen her that animated." His intrigued gaze dipped to Blythe's, and a sensation much like warm silk caressed her. "Thank you. She needs kind friends."

"She's sweet. I'm going to speak with Brooke about taking her under our wing." Blythe regarded him candidly. "If you're amenable to the suggestion."

"Miss Culpepper, I would be immensely grateful."

To her surprise, they'd reached the dance floor. Why, if they continued to speak of Francine, the waltz might be bearable after all.

"I bumped into Mr. Phillips upstairs. I believe he'd been sequestered in an alcove with Miss Sanford. She left Francine in the ladies retiring room, and spoke rather unkindly to her."

"No surprise there. Miss Sanford's friendship with my cousin is prompted by ulterior motives." An elusive emotion shadowed his lordship's eyes, deepening the blue to cerulean. "Phillips wasn't forward with you, was he? He's ..." He bent his head as they took their place upon the floor. "He's a disreputable sort."

His concern surprised and touched her. Perhaps Brooke was right, and Lord Leventhorpe possessed a heart after all. "I gathered as much. He attempted to extract my given name. I refused."

The waltz began, and Blythe dipped into a curtsy as his lordship bowed, his unusual lion's head stickpin in the folds of his cravat catching her eye. Its ruby eyes and diamond mouth twinkled in the incandescent light. A family heirloom?

Stepping into his embrace wasn't what Blythe had anticipated either. Though not as light on his feet as Mr. Burlington, Lord Leventhorpe proved a superb dancer, especially for such a towering man. She frequently stood taller than men and quite liked having to look upward to meet his eyes.

Mr. Burlington had been on eye level with her.

So?

Like the muscular statues in the entry, his lordship's shoulder was thick and rounded, the sinewy flesh flexing beneath her fingertips. What other parts of his anatomy might be as generous? Heat stole up her cheeks, and her breathing sputtered for a moment.

Oh, for the love of God, Blythe. Stop.

Of a slimmer build, Mr. Burlington had been solid, but didn't boast the marquis's bulging physique.

Nothing wrong with that. He wasn't scrawny or

twitchy like Mr. Phillips, repulsive man.

She and Lord Leventhorpe danced well together, their forms nicely proportioned. As they rose and fell to the orchestra's strains, his lordship's subtle scent wafted to her. Swaying in his arms, she took a deep breath. In addition to his usual sandalwood, Blythe detected cloves and fresh linen. And perhaps a hint of brandy?

Mr. Burlington's cologne had been musky.

Both smelled pleasant, yet distinctly different, like the men themselves.

Stop comparing them, for pity's sake.

Lord Leventhorpe fell silent once their dance began, and the delight of being held in his strong embrace was unexpected and disconcerting. A month ago, she'd have believed herself dicked in the nob for entertaining such an absurd notion as enjoying a waltz with him.

Did his thoughts run parallel to hers, confusion meshed with pleasure? She entertained no misconceptions about his prior sentiments toward her.

Blythe slanted her head, and her gaze collided with his half-open sapphire eyes, the tips of his lashes feathered auburn. She stumbled, mashing his toes.

Had he observed her while they circled the floor?

The gentle upward sweep of his mouth sent a

frisson to the tips of her toes, and she missed another step. So much for confidence in her dance skills.

He drew her infinitesimally closer, though surely only because of her momentary clumsiness.

She ought to object, but her tongue seemed content to stay silent.

Say something.

"Francine says you take her riding."

His attention dropped to Blythe's mouth before he nodded. "Yes. When I'm able. Because we prefer the park to ourselves, I collect her at seven o'clock."

The music ended, and after a hesitant moment, he released her and gave a short bow.

Well, that hadn't been unpleasant at all.

Blythe curtsied then accepted his arm as she searched amongst the crush for her family. Encountering several hastily averted, speculative gazes, she fought a smile.

Quite a number of busybodies in attendance.

His lordship escorted her to their bench, albeit by a circuitous route. "If you would like to join us, I'm sure Francine would be delighted."

At the nearness of his mouth to her ear, Blythe gave a start. He seemed particularly fond of doing that.

"Alas, I fear I don't ride sidesaddle. I never learned how. There wasn't a need at Esherton Green,

THE MARQUIS AND THE VIXEN

nor much opportunity with an old nag fit only for our dogcart." She pulled a face and gestured with her fan. "But I think we must learn now. It's expected, isn't it?"

"Usually, not always. I don't think anyone should be forced to do something they find objectionable." A peculiar inflection entered his voice, and a flash of pain glinted in his eyes for an instant.

With considerable effort, she dragged her gaze from his and located her family.

Mr. Burlington waited with Brooke and Heath. The girls' escorts must have already claimed them for the supper dance. Unaccustomed to dancing all evening, Blythe's feet had grown sore, and she welcomed the opportunity to sit for a while.

As if reluctant to relinquish her, Lord Leventhorpe slowed his pace. "Miss Culpepper, I would be happy to teach you to ride sidesaddle. If you would like to learn."

The man was full of surprises tonight. What next?

A warbling love sonnet for a shy wallflower?

A race through The Green Park in his underthings?

No, he was too taciturn for either, but his unexpected offer touched her.

"You have a sweet-tempered mare and a

sidesaddle tucked in your London mews, my lord?" She wasn't going to learn to stay balanced atop that ridiculous contraption while seated astride a giant of a horse. Men should be made to ride on the stupid thing since they insisted ladies do so. No, a sedate pony or donkey would do perfectly until she mastered the skill. "I cannot conceive of you seated upon either. I've seen that immense, russet brute you ride. That beast looks to be descended from a mythological creature."

She grinned at his flummoxed expression. He didn't know she jested. Lord Leventhorpe was too serious by far.

"I raised Bucephalus from a foal." He summoned a grin and scratched his nose. "Buce is named after Alexander the Great's gargantuan steed, said to have had an immense head."

"A most fitting name." They had nearly reached the others. "You've other horseflesh in London too?"

"I have several horses and carriages at a local livery. Raven asked me to let him know if I spotted horseflesh appropriate for women at Tattersalls, and last week, a brilliant mare caught my eye. Perhaps you'd care to accompany me to the auction tomorrow to view the mare?"

And now an offer of an outing? Blythe rather liked this Lord Leventhorpe.

"I'd like to, and the others may want to attend also. That way we can see if the mare suits before Heath purchases her. Is it permissible? I didn't think women were allowed."

"If you are in my and Ravensdale's company, it's acceptable." Lord Leventhorpe lifted a shoulder. "If he doesn't purchase the mare, I shall. She's a rare beauty sporting a champagne coat with a creamy white mane and tail."

"Oh, she sounds gorgeous. Heath has suggested we wait until we return to the country to learn to ride, but, I confess, I crave the outdoors and would adore early morning jaunts. I used to take a lengthy walk with Freddy at dawn each day."

He slanted his brow. "Never had a beast detest me more than that aged, gone-to-fat corgi."

"Brooke thinks your cologne set the dog against you at Esherton. A man wearing a similar fragrance abused him. At the end, Freddy warmed to you." She dropped her hand as they reached the bench. She'd like the feel of his solid forearm flexing beneath her fingertips. "Brooke, Lord Leventhorpe has generously offered to teach us to ride sidesaddle."

An exuberant grin lit Mr. Burlington's face. "One of my greatest pleasures is riding, and I would enjoy sharing the experience with you. That is, if

Leventhorpe doesn't object."

The look in his eyes warmed Blythe to her mistreated toes. A handsome man's admiration did bolster one's confidence, yet the intensity in Lord Leventhorpe's gaze while they danced meant more.

Probably because he didn't loathe her any longer. No one relished being disliked.

Mr. Burlington turned his affable gaze to his lordship. "Leventhorpe, would I be imposing? I helped teach my three younger sisters, and would be happy to volunteer my time and services."

"Not at all, Burlington. Unless Ravensdale prefers the ladies wait." Lord Leventhorpe's tone belied his words. Over her head, he regarded Heath, and as certain as Freddy had peed on Heath's boot at Esherton, a silent message passed between them.

She'd done that very thing with her sister and cousins myriad times.

Enough doubt niggled to steal her earlier enthusiasm about the lessons. She cast Lord Leventhorpe a glance, and her heart flipped when she caught him regarding her. What she wouldn't give to read his thoughts.

Was he considering reneging because Mr. Burlington offered to help? That made no sense. She would think he'd welcome another hand. None of the

Culpeppers had ever sat a sidesaddle. Though the task might prove considerable, they might as well learn here as at home. And she would be assured of time with Mr. Burlington, affording her the opportunity to become better acquainted. More importantly, riding lessons meant escaping the house and spending time in the outdoors, and after her stay in London, both appealed more than either man.

Liar.

Enough. She refused to examine her musings further.

"I think Lord Leventhorpe may have taken on more than he wagered, and I'm sure he would appreciate any assistance he can gather, Mr. Burlington. I'm quite looking forward to learning, aren't you, Brooke?" Clasping her hands, and painting a bright smile upon her face, Blythe turned to Lord Leventhorpe. "Is the day after tomorrow too soon to begin lessons?"

Though circumstances appear to
confirm schemes laid in advance, when motives
are selfish, expect unforeseen and unpleasant results.
~*Dignity and Decorum—The Genteel Lady's
Guide to Practical Living*

"*T*here he is.*" Tristan pointed to Hawksworth
slumped atop a lopsided table in a fusty
corner. "Looks practically pickled.*"

"*What's he doing in The Ship & Whistle?*"
*Ravensdale surveyed the unsavory establishment
through the grungy window.*

"*Probably assumed we wouldn't look here. It's a
favorite of sailors and servicemen. Cheap prostitutes
and cheaper spirits.*" Tristan dipped his head as they
entered the tavern, the stench of unwashed bodies,
sweat, vomit, and spilled ale causing a reflexive surge
of bile.*

"*Ho there, Ravensdale. Leventhorpe.*" Phillips

and a handful of his cronies, all foxed to the gills, stumbled into the establishment. "Come to hire a wench for the evening too?"

Never fastidious or selective, Phillips had retained a flaxen-haired running-to-fat tavern harlot. He pinched her full buttocks. "We can share her, can't we, darlin'?"

She leaned into him. "Sure, guv.'"

"No. We cannot." Tristan glowered at Phillips.

Ravensdale shook his head. "I'll pass."

Tristan and Ravensdale each, for entirely different reasons, never entertained light skirts.

"What about Hawksworth? That Friday face looks like he could use a bit of cheering." Phillips's jibe earned him a blank, glassy-eyed stare from Hawk.

"M' lifesh ended now anyway." Hawksworth's slurred speech testified to his drunk-as-a-wheelbarrow condition. "Might ashh well 'urry i' along." Grinning sloppily, he squinted and tried to focus. "Where ish she?"

Ape drunk, Hawksworth wasn't capable of a cockstand.

He wasn't capable of standing at all.

"At least one of you three ba a working set of ballocks." Slapping his chest, Phillips chortled and grabbed Hawksworth's arm. "Come on, man. Let's get

you upstairs, unless you want to take her here." He slid Tristan a sly look. "Some men enjoy an audience."

Tristan clamped his jaw and balled his hands, sweat beading his upper lip and soaking his armpits. Had Phillips learned of his humiliation? Zounds. How?

Phillips turned to the harlot. "You don't mind, do you, Shelly, sweetheart?"

She grinned, revealing a mouth of yellowed teeth, and drew her grungy, stained blouse low on her sagging breasts. "Naw, makes i' more fun. I charges extra fer peepers, though."

"Up with you, Hawksworth." Phillips tugged Hawk's arm again, attempting to rouse him from his chair and stupor. "Shelly knows her trade and several unique tricks too. You'll not be disappointed."

Bloody eager to watch, pervert.

"Leave him be. Unlike you, he isn't keen on acquiring the pox." Ravensdale glowered at Seymour and his comrades, who'd formed a taunting semicircle around them.

Seven to three. Not the best odds.

Hawksworth slouched with his eyes closed and chin slack against his chest. Make that two. Rather dismal chances, actually. Couldn't be helped.

Shoving Phillips's hand away from Hawk, Tristan

sliced Ravensdale a silent message. "We want no part of your doxy."

"Wot's wrong wif ye, luv?" The strumpet sidled up to Tristan, her foul odor revolting. From her stench, she'd already been busy this evening. She rubbed against him, releasing another unpleasant whiff of her unwashed body.

Queasiness twisted his stomach tighter.

"Ya prefer tuppin' gents?"

Doubled up with glee, Phillips choked on his laughter, his drunken entourage also guffawing.

"You haven't always felt that way, Leventhorpe." Phillips grinned nastily and scratched his groin. "I seem to recall something my father let slip. Something your father shared at Brooks's while deep in his cups one day."

Father was usually in his cups.

"Stubble it, Phillips." Ravensdale dragged his hand through his hair, compassion tinting the gaze he sent Tristan.

He and Hawksworth, alone, were privy to the event that haunted Tristan, and they didn't know the whole of it. He had never been able to speak of the horrific humiliation.

"Wasn't there an instance when you had quite a public display of lust, Leventhorpe?" Phillips held up

two fingers. "One that involved two prostitutes?"
Tristan's well-placed facer broke Phillips's nose.

Tristan bolted upright, cursing and disoriented. Darkness enveloped him, and for an instant, he didn't know where he was.

God.

He rubbed his face before lying down once more.

A nightmare. Not his usual, though.

Pure fate, Whitehouse and Drake had happened along that evening, in time to prevent Ravensdale and Tristan from getting completely thrashed. They had jumped into the ensuing fray, balancing the odds nicely. The five had been the greatest of chums ever since.

Nothing quite like fighting side-by-side against a common foe to forge unbreakable bonds of friendship. A week later, they'd shared mutual misgivings too, when the same diseased slattern, tortured and beaten to death, washed ashore on the River Thames's beach.

Tristan closed his eyes against his musing and the accompanying disquiet. He kicked off his bedcovers, and after punching his pillow into an acceptable shape, flopped onto his stomach.

Slumber didn't embrace him.

The rhythmic *tick-tocking* of his bedside table clock usually lulled him to sleep. He cracked an eye open and glared at the indiscernible oval face in the pre-dawn half-light.

What time was it?

Too early to rise, by half.

He hadn't heard a peep from Peasley, and the valet took particular pleasure in slinging open the window coverings the moment the first ray of sun brazened the horizon.

In the distance, a dog barked, and a moment later, an answering woof sounded.

Yawning, Tristan stretched his legs, encountering several furry paws despite his mammoth mattress. Clio and Thalia sprawled at the foot of his bed, softly snoring and twitching every now and again.

He ought to make them get off the bed.

Despite regular brushing, the dogs shed terribly, and White's chambermaid fretted when she had to clean the collies' hair from the coverlet and furniture. The extra vails Tristan offered for her inconvenience lessened her vexation a jot. More than once, he'd endured his valet's wrath as Peasley tutted and fussed while ridding Tristan's togs of hair before permitting him to present himself in public.

For the first time, Tristan had stayed until a ball's confounded end—very nearly a miracle thanks to the humiliating experience his despot of a father had foisted upon him at thirteen.

Wide awake and agitated after last night's ball, he hadn't found his bed until after half past two. Yet each time he shut his eyelids, a halo of silvery hair, violet-blue eyes below delicate honey-blond brows, a pert nose, and stubborn chin taunted him. He'd been hard-put not to stare at the firm teacup-sized bosoms teasing her bodice's neckline during their waltz. He'd fallen into an agitated slumber only to have Phillips encroach upon his dreams.

He didn't trust Phillip's, and Burlington's interest in Blythe chaffed worse than a week bare-arsed in a new saddle, though why it should confounded Tristan.

Worry and concern.

That was what this unease centered in his gut was. None of his blasted business, by God. The Culpeppers weren't—Blythe most assuredly wasn't—his concern.

Stop thinking about her, and go to sleep.

His rebellious musings ignored him.

Tristan had told Ravensdale about Blythe's unnerving upstairs encounter with Phillips, and evidently, Raven had conveyed their mutual disquiet to his wife.

For the evening's remainder, Lady Ravensdale had insisted the Culpeppers visit the retiring room *en masse*. Until they became familiar with *haut ton* protocol, and accumulated a set of trustworthy friends, Tristan applauded her decision.

Years of experience guiding the tightknit quartet would serve her, and them, well in London. Tristan admired the Culpeppers' unity. Genuinely kind and friendly, they'd soon have a circle of supporters.

Surely Ravensdale's melon had gone soft for descending upon London with his new family in tow. With that lot churning High Society's staid waters, Tristan might have enjoyed this Season. However, his abhorrence of crowds prevented any such thing. His habit of imbibing a couple of stiff drinks before venturing to a gathering sufficed when he did so once a fortnight at most.

But, *damn my eyes,* Ravensdale had asked for his help, which meant multiple forays weekly.

Mayhap Tristan would purchase a barrel of whisky. He shook his face in his crisp pillowcase's folds. No. He'd not end up a fuddled drunkard like his father.

Then you need to find another way to deal with your dread.

Grunting, Tristan turned onto his back and stared at the inky canopy. He scratched his bare chest before tucking his hands underneath his head.

Promising to teach the Culpeppers to ride.

Had *his* melon gone soft?

Now he'd have to bear Burlington's insufferable presence too. He wanted to hate the man, but couldn't. Not for being a favorite with the ladies and taking advantage of what many offered freely. Tristan, Heath, and Hawksworth were anomalies in that regard, though they weren't monks, just exceedingly selective.

Well ... Heath had been prior to marriage. Now, tits over arse in love, Raven would never betray Lady Ravensdale.

The epitome of discretion when it came to his dalliances, much like Drake and Whitehouse, Burlington didn't possess despicable habits. He came from a long line of respectable peers, and the Earl of Lauderdale was an upright chap, if a bit thin in the pockets. Other than a weak constitution, Burlington's older brother boasted an exemplary character too.

Damme.

Burlington had to have one unsavory practice. He was too bloody perfect by far. Only his lack of title made him less desirable to some women. Others mightn't care.

Did Blythe?

She wasn't the sort, which made Burlington more of a threat.

Clio twitched and whined in her sleep. Probably dreamed of running the fields and herding the cattle at Bristledale. Tristan should have left the dogs there, but truthfully, he missed them and found London lonely.

The blame for that, too, could be plopped at his doorstep.

A stack of unopened invitations lay piled atop the corner secretary where he'd tossed them.

He didn't relish returning to his empty rooms at White's, and since he stayed in most evenings—at least he had until this confounded Season—he found the dogs welcome company. True, he'd rented these quarters for a decade, and they bore his personal touch and preferences, but the pleasant rooms weren't home.

Only at Bristledale Court, away from Town's observant eyes, attending ears, and flapping tongues, did he find a degree of respite.

As for the house bearing witness to his disgrace as a youth, he'd have sold the place and its furnishings for a pittance without an iota of regret within a week of inheriting the marquisate if the damned thing weren't entailed. He couldn't bear to pass the residence and went out of his way to avoid the street altogether.

No matter how many times he told himself what had happened those many years ago wasn't his fault, he couldn't rid himself of the dirty, used feeling. And with Phillips's return, more people might soon know of his degradation.

A thirteen-year-old, even one the size of a grown man, should never be forced to have his first sexual encounter with jaded prostitutes reeking of cheap perfume, and witnessed by debauched lechers. He'd tried to resist, but against the women's well-honed skills, he'd battled in vain. Even as his mind screeched no, and he'd pleaded and screamed for them to stop, his healthy, young body on the cusp of manhood had responded.

Growling deep in his chest, Tristan flopped a bent arm across his face, as if to hide the scene replaying behind his eyes for the thousandth time. The whores' appreciative coos and laughter mixed with the men's vile remarks regarding his immediate and impressive erection echoed in his dreams.

In his waking hours too.

His stomach roiled, and his nostrils twitched. He'd never forget the putrid smells either.

When a sodomite had asked to have him, and his sire drunkenly agreed, Tristan fought loose of the men restraining him. After he broke the bugger's groping hand, he'd fled the house and stayed either at school or as a guest of chums until he acquired his own lodgings at eighteen.

He never saw his father again.

Not even upon his deathbed, when Father repented of his lifetime of depravity and sent word, begging Tristan to visit him in order to make amends before he died. Better that his sire had changed his ways and sought reconciliation and forgiveness when he had time to make restitution. Precisely like the selfish, old marquis to lay the burden of forgiveness on Tristan.

Why should he grant Father forgiveness?

So he could enter eternal slumber with a contented heart and pure conscience? Hawksworth had argued, many times, that forgiving Father would bring healing and peace.

Tristan's loud snort rent the heavy silence, and Thalia raised her head, giving a weak woof.

He would never have peace. Not while he drew breath.

Every day for the past fifteen years, he'd striven for that elusive state. Just when he thought he'd made progress, that he'd finally put the taunting shadows to rest, something stirred them again. Like Phillips last night. And to know Father had spoken of the incident ... How many of the others present had as well?

Tristan gave a savage groan. Devil and damn. The lot, no doubt. His distance from *ton* activities had protected him from the bitter knowledge.

Thomas Gray had it right. *"Where ignorance is bliss, 'tis folly to be wise."*

Thalia lifted her head when Tristan made another inarticulate sound of revulsion.

By God, when he had children—*if* he had children—he'd be a decent father, far superior to his sire. A deuced better husband too.

Clio crawled up his side then laid her pointed muzzle atop his chest.

The dogs sensed his distress.

Tristan ran a hand down her spine. "I suppose you think I should walk you?" She thumped her tail once. "You do realize I'll have to tie my cravat myself?" Two more thumps and a whine confirmed the dog's need.

Thirty minutes later—Peasley would have apoplexy when he discovered Tristan's rudimentarily tied neckcloth—Tristan slipped his arms into his greatcoat. A serving boy had taken the dogs out while he had eaten a hasty breakfast. For expediency, Tristan had stuffed bacon between the croissants flaky folds before gulping two strong cups of Turkish coffee. After a sleepless night, he'd need the restorative beverage to keep him alert today.

After snapping leads onto the dogs' collars, he collected his cane and made his way outside to his waiting landau.

"Good morning, my lord. Your paper." Jones passed the news sheet to Tristan then stepped to hold the carriage door open. The morning proved brisk, though the first rays of sunshine glinting off the vehicle's azure paint, promised a temperate day later. "The ladies are energetic early, I see."

"Good morning, Jones." Tristan wedged the paper beneath his arm and passed the leads to the driver before stepping into the landau. "They were most insistent we have an early constitutional today."

At his whistle, the dogs bounded into the conveyance. Hopping onto the opposite, blanket-covered seat, they raised their pointed snouts and sniffed. London's air seldom lacked for odors.

"The Green Park as usual, your lordship?" Jones asked as he snapped the reins and, with a slight lurch, the vehicle rolled forward.

"Yes." Crossing his legs, Tristan pulled the folded news sheet free. He skimmed the first pages. Nothing original or fresh. Just the same drudgery rewritten from a different perspective than yesterday's. And the day before's. He'd grown weary of the rhetoric already, and Parliament wouldn't recess soon. *More's the pity.*

Squinting as the conveyance turned in the sun, he scratched his nose. Hiring someone to vote in proxy didn't appeal. Granted, many peers condoned the practice, but until he had reason—other than loathing London—to avoid Parliamentary proceedings, he'd not abdicate his responsibilities.

Clio jumped onto the seat beside Tristan, sending his cane clattering to the floor. Her claws digging into his thigh to stay balanced, she shoved her wet nose underneath the paper, knocking several sheets loose to join his cane. Tail happily wagging, she licked his cheek.

"No. Clio." He pointed to her sister. "You belong there. Off with you."

Head lowered, Clio did as bidden. Lying across the opposite seat, her muzzle resting upon her paws, she watched him soulfully.

"Don't look at me like that. Peasley will have my head if he finds a single strand of dog hair upon my clothing, and I have several calls to make before I can return to my lodgings. Would you have me disparaged?"

She licked her chops, her tail twitching.

As he bent to retrieve his cane and the scattered news sheets, his attention fell upon the natter column.

Such claptrap was good for the rubbish bin, a fireplace, or picking up after the dogs' occasional accidents.

He scanned the neat print.

London's first formal glimpse of Ldy R and the four Ms Cs caused a considerable stir last evening. ... Mr. B showed a distinct penchant for the elder Ms C, much to the disappointment of many a fair maid.

He was one gentleman amongst many to pay marked attention to the five diamonds of the first water. Even the reclusive Ld L put in an unexpected, coveted appearance.

No matter how well-intended or
magnificent the scheme, one should
occasionally consider the consequences.
~*Dignity and Decorum—The Genteel Lady's
Guide to Practical Living*

5

Tristan snatched the paper from the floor.

*One has to wonder if Ld L has finally decided to
pursue matrimony with one of the newly arrived blond
beauties.*

No. He most emphatically had not.

*This columnist means to watch Society's reaction
and predicts the thwarting of many a well-laid
scheme...*

Tristan checked an annoyed grunt and seized his

cane. The silver lion's head grip hid a sword handle. He never ventured anywhere on foot without the weapon.

Once he gathered the news sheets into an untidy pile, he laid them beside his leg.

A rather tame assessment and not altogether contrived, discounting the nonsensical twaddle about Tristan pursuing matrimony. Relaxing into the seat, he tapped his fingers on the landau's side as they neared the park.

How long did Raven expect him to help with his newly acquired family?

Tristan could cry off. Except ... he reluctantly admitted to a perverse fascination. He might be almost as eager to see what High Society made of the ladies as Ravensdale.

Le beau monde could be as fickle as a Friday night whore, and her favors bought as easily. All the more reason to be nearby, in case this ill-hatched scheme unraveled.

Tristan would arrange the riding lesson details after calling and collecting whichever of the young ladies wanted to venture to Tattersalls. The landau rolled to a stop and, after alighting and untangling the dogs' leashes, Tristan grabbed his cane. Taking a refreshing breath, he set a brisk pace toward

Constitution Hill, waving for Jones to collect him on the other side, as he did each morning.

Whistling softly, Tristan mentally catalogued the day's priorities.

He should call upon Francine and, again, advise her about her choice of companions. Blythe, her sisters, and her cousins were exactly the type of friends Francine needed—kind, decent women—not the string of ambitious chits who continually used Francine for their gain.

Farther along the lane, a short-legged bundle of fur-covered fat pelted between two gnarled trees chasing a cow in desperate need of milking.

A cacophony of shouting, barking, and mooing echoed throughout the park. Ears perked in excited interest, Clio and Thalia tugged at their leashes, tails wagging furiously.

"Freddy. Stop."

"Come back, ya ruddy beasty."

"Stop, Clover. I needs t' milk ye."

Tristan faced the racket's direction.

Blythe, a pink and white confection, her bonnet's ribbons trailing behind her, tore across the green followed by a milkmaid, her skirts yanked to her knees, and a lad clenching a rope in one hand and holding his cap atop his head with the other.

Ah, a bovine escapee from adjacent St. James Park's milk lines, and the Culpeppers' corgi loved to herd cattle. Tristan wagered the little devil hadn't been able to resist the runaway cow.

A teenage groom sprinted past Blythe, slicing a diagonal path, intent on cutting the panicked cow off. Another man, noticing the ruckus, gave chase as well, and beyond him, another chap moved toward the animal, though at a more sedate pace.

Pulling his hat lower, the latter abruptly turned in the opposite direction and proceeded to briskly walk away.

With the sun shining in his eyes, Tristan couldn't make him out. Perhaps he'd decided his help wasn't needed to capture the panicked beast. A wonder she didn't knock her hind hooves from beneath her with her bulging udders wildly careening like kettle-sized, milk-filled clappers.

Tristan whistled an imitation of one he'd heard the overseer at Esherton Green use with Freddy. He immediately whirled and trotted Tristan's way, his tongue nearly dragging the pavement along with his leash. Failing eyesight and the distance contributed to the dog's inability to recognize Tristan.

Wait until you realize it's me. You'll be off the other direction faster than angels fleeing hell.

The cow continued to dash along, her enormous udders making Tristan wince with each swing.

Thank God he wasn't a milk cow.

Sunshine, golden and bright, filtered through the tree-lined lane, casting interwoven shadows along the path. He bent and, after unclipping Clio's and Thalia's leashes, pointed at the cow. "Fetch."

Panting, her hair flopping onto one shoulder and her bonnet askew, Blythe dashed onto the pavement. Freddy, a doggy grin splitting his gray face, waddled to her. "Naughty boy. Chasing poor Clover."

Tristan approached cautiously. He didn't need the dog tearing off in a panic too. Squatting, he extended a hand. "Hello, Freddy. There's a good chap."

Freddy skulked closer, his haunches practically hugging the ground and sniffed timidly. He licked Tristan's fingertips then peered at Blythe for approval.

Swiping at a tendril tickling her cheek, Blythe crouched, the graceful curve of her mouth sweeping into a pleased grin. "Well done, Freddy." Patting the dog, she seized his lead and turned a brilliant smile upon Tristan. "He doesn't fear you any longer."

"The wayward cow has been caught." Tristan steered his gaze behind her.

Looking over her shoulder, she stood. "I was about to enjoy a cup of fresh milk when a rail-thin urchin startled Clover." Melancholy riddled her voice. "I felt a jot homesick, and the cows reminded me of Esherton Green. I milked cows almost daily at home." She shook her head, causing a few more curls to tumble loose, and gave a little self-deprecating laugh. "I don't suppose that's altogether ladylike."

"I quite enjoy a cup of fresh milk." Not exactly the fact. He did claim a particular fondness for clotted cream and milk in his coffee. Fresh from the cow's teat, and drunk from a communal cup? No. He managed to conceal his miniscule repugnance-born tremor.

The lad led the docile beast, the rope now circling Clover's thick neck, while the milkmaid, obviously his sister given the smattering of freckles also covering her broad face, guided the cow with a hand to her black and white dappled neck.

Thalia and Clio trotted behind, a safe distance from the cow's hind legs, and the groom and other gentleman brought up the rear.

"Miss, I'm afeared I left the cup yonder. To thank ye fer yer help, I'd be pleased to give ye a drink fer no cost ifn ye want to walk back." The girl repeatedly glanced in the vicinity of connecting St. James Park. "It were kind of ye to give the beggar child yer blunt."

Did a father, or perhaps an employer, expect the

milkmaid? Would the children be chastised for the loss of a sale? Tristan passed the lad a shilling and the lass two. "You each keep a coin. The other is to pay for the sales you've lost."

The boy's face lit like fireworks above Vauxhall Gardens. He bobbed his moppy head. "Thank ye, m'lord."

"Thank ye, again, fer yer help, m'lord. Miss. Gents." After pocketing her coins and attempting a clumsy curtsy, the milkmaid headed for St. James Park, her brother chatting and gesturing excitedly about what he intended to buy with his money.

"That was kind of you, my lord." With a soft sigh, Blythe turned to her groom as Freddy and the collies sniffed one another in greeting. "Bennett, would you please fetch the carriage?"

Endeavoring to remedy the havoc her adventure had caused to her hair, she shoved a clump below her bonnet. Holding the hat in place, she tucked a few more strands underneath the brim. After tying the ribbons, she brushed ineffectually at her dress. "I fear I must repair my appearance before anyone else comes upon me this disheveled."

Charmingly tousled, she'd never looked lovelier to Tristan.

Stains marred the palms of her gloves, and grass

smeared her gown's front near her knees. One long green streak emphasized the delicious mounds of her plump buttocks, testifying to a tumble or two as she chased the cow.

Uneasiness snuffed his appreciation.

God's toenails. Had anyone else seen her?

Tristan stretched to his full height and canvassed the vista. No one in sight. Not even the fellow who'd decided against helping earlier.

Thank the ungodly hour for the park's solitude. Why had Blythe ventured out this early with only a young stable hand for a chaperone? Most imprudent. Doubtless, besotted by her beauty, the whelp hadn't been able to deny her request, despite possibly risking discharge.

She wouldn't want word spread about that she'd been seen with grass-stained skirts. Foul minds might speculate that someone had given her a green gown, and she certainly didn't want the tattlemongers whispering she'd been tumbled in the park.

Likely as not, Raven wasn't aware Blythe had ventured out. A conversation with him seemed judicious. Not altogether safe for her if the man who'd abruptly departed was who Tristan suspected.

"Leventhorpe, is that you?" Wiping perspiration from his brow with his handkerchief, the fellow who'd succeeded in stopping the cow grinned at Tristan.

"Clancy Maddox?" Tristan extended his hand. "By George. It's been a long time. What, ten years or more? Not since university."

"Eleven." He sent Blythe a curious glance. "I was two years ahead of you."

"Allow me to present you." Tristan made the introductions before leashing his dogs.

"Thank you for your assistance, Mr. Maddox." Blythe picked up Freddy. The panting dog sagged against her, tuckered from his jaunt.

Women of refined breeding didn't tote portly corgis about, or run pell-mell through The Green Park. Another thing he needed to address with Lady Ravensdale and Raven. What Blythe might have been free to do in the country would be frowned upon in Town and could lead to wagging tongues. Something they didn't want if they wished successful come-outs.

Sure as fish guts stank, Blythe didn't care.

Kissing the top of Freddy's head, she shifted the dog, and her reticule slid to her wrist. "He thinks he's young, and though he tried to help with the runaway cow, I fear he did more harm than good."

"Where are you staying, Maddox? Are you here for a while?" Tristan jammed his cane between his side and arm then took the dog from her. Freddy eyed him warily, yet after a moment, laid his head upon Tristan's shoulder and released a long, throaty sigh.

So much for not wearing dog hair today.

"I've let rooms on St. James Street." Maddox placed his hat tighter upon his head. "I'm considering staying and opening an office here. A decade in the colonies was long enough for me. The provincials lack England's refinement and culture."

They reached the lane's end as Ravensdale's carriage drew to a stop behind Tristan's landau. A third conveyance leisurely eased past, the team clopping at a sedate pace. The collies loped to Tristan's vehicle, and in a moment, tongues lolling, sat perched atop the seat peering expectantly at him.

Maddox tipped his hat. "It was a pleasure to meet you, Miss Culpepper. I bid you good day."

"Likewise." She fished a card from her reticule. "Please come for tea tomorrow. I wish to thank you properly. This is my cousin-in-law's card. Mine are at the printers."

His brows dipped together as he read the card. "Ravensdale? I wasn't aware he'd wed recently."

"Yes." Cinching her reticule's handle, she turned somewhat away from another slow-passing carriage. "He married my cousin a short time ago."

"Thank you for the invitation to tea." He bowed to

Blythe. "I look forward to seeing Ravensdale and meeting his bride."

She nodded a farewell as she made for her carriage.

Awkwardly balancing Freddy and worriedly watching Blythe's retreating form, Tristan shook Maddox's hand. "I lodge at White's. Be sure to look me up."

"I shall." Maddox's gaze gravitated to Blythe. "Will I see you at tea as well, Leventhorpe?"

"I expect so." Tristan canted his head in Blythe's direction. "There are five of them, and Raven's asked me to make myself available to assist with that tribe of beauties."

"Five? *Five?*" Maddox chuckled and shook his head. "Egads, that ought to be something. Glad I'm back in time to see it, I am."

"A common consensus, my friend." Tristan gave a conspiratorial wink.

"Till tomorrow then." With a carefree wave, Maddox, swinging his cane, headed in the direction he'd come.

Careful to keep his staff secured underneath his arm, Tristan adjusted a now-drowsy Freddy.

How much did the little piglet weigh?

A pair of carriages rumbled past, their occupants

craning their necks, no doubt curious who else dared the common at this unchristian hour. The park appeared to be a favorite destination for those enjoying an early morning constitutional today.

He deposited the leashes in his landau and gave instructions to Jones before meeting Blythe at her carriage.

Arms akimbo and one toe tapping, she considered Maddox's retreating form. She turned her puckish regard upon Tristan, pinning him with her direct gaze. "You made it sound like Heath's taken on a Herculean task." Pique sharpened her features and voice. "We're not that difficult."

"I didn't imply *you* were. It's the rest of the upper ten-thousand—London actually—that will be difficult to manage. They've never encountered anything like the Culpeppers." He chuckled, and answering humor sparked in her eyes.

"I can well imagine." She scratched behind Freddy's ears, and he opened an eye. "I think you've found a friend."

"He's a good sort." Tristan patted Freddy's haunch and bent his head toward the groom standing ready to hand her into the carriage. "That was well done of you back there."

"Thank you, m'lord." He grinned at Blythe. "I

thought Miss Culpepper would outpace me. Never seen a lady run that fast."

"See what I mean?" Tristan whispered in her ear, delighting in the blush infusing her cheeks as she entered the carriage

She extended her arms for Freddy. He groaned and scrambled onto the seat, where he promptly curled into a ball.

Tristan signaled Jones, and with an understanding slant of his head, the driver clicked his tongue and flexed the reins.

"I'll accompany you. I need to speak with Ravensdale." Before she could object with a single syllable, Tristan stepped in right behind her and shut the door with a portentous thunk. He stretched his legs before him. "Pray tell, what were you doing gamboling around London before an acceptable hour with a stable lad as chaperone?"

Scheming seldom results in anything extraordinary
or eternal, for anything worth having is freely given.
~Dignity and Decorum—The Genteel Lady's
Guide to Practical Living

6

"My lord, I assure you, you needn't accompany me, and I wasn't 'gamboling' around London. I merely sought to walk Freddy in the park, as it appeared, you also intended with your collies." Blythe ground her teeth in vexation as she settled against the toast-gold, velvet squabs. That she managed to speak and not snipe or shout brought her a modicum of satisfaction. "And Bennet is perfectly acceptable for a chaperone."

Wasn't he? Should she have brought her maid too? She hadn't bothered with that sort of propriety in the country, where the only things that might set upon her were a stray cat or disgruntled crow.

"A peer walking his large dogs, a short sword

concealed within his walking stick," Lord Leventhorpe indicated the elaborate staff tucked into the corner by his seat, "is deuced sure safer than a maiden with a fuzzy, waddling walrus and a smitten stable hand, scarcely more than a wet-behind-the-ears lad, for protection."

His cutting wit drew blood, and that he spoke the truth rankled. Nearly blind and missing several teeth, Freddy, the epitome of decrepitude, offered as much protection as the one-eyed stuffed pheasant in Esherton's study.

Picking dog hair from her spencer, she surreptitiously studied Lord Leventhorpe. Alternating sunbeams and shadows filtered through the windows as the carriage rolled past the row of impressive trees. The light played over his rugged features, making it impossible to read his expression.

Austere or staid? Mayhap somber? Taciturn? Grave?

Definitely not giddy. *Never* giddy.

Despite her frustration, a smile tickled her mouth.

Had he deduced she'd left without notifying anyone and decided to take it upon himself to tell them?

Quite possibly.

That fit the self-righteous, overbearing lord she'd

met at Esherton. The amiable, enjoyable man of last night had vanished with the moon and stars' disappearance, and the sanctimonious lord, the one who believed it his duty to inform others of their shortcomings, had returned. Weren't demons supposed to prowl about at night and slink into their dank and gloomy hidey-holes at first light, not the reverse?

Did he think her a wholly inconsiderate bacon wit? She'd left a note with Jenkin, their butler, saying she'd gone for a walk, for pity's sake. Suppressing an urge to kick Lord Leventhorpe, she pressed her half-boot's heel against the seat and petted Freddy instead.

Despite her late night, she'd awoken at dawn, a habit she'd not overcome from years of rising early at Esherton. Desperate to escape the house's confines and London's cramped busyness, she'd sought refuge in the singular place remotely resembling Esherton Green. Her sisters—everyone, barring Cook—had been abed when she'd slipped to the mews. Bennet, alone, prowled the stables, and she'd bade him ready a conveyance and accompany her to the park.

He'd eagerly agreed, much preferring that task to mucking the stalls. Biting the inside of her mouth, she pressed her fingers into Freddy's pudgy back. Would her impulsiveness result in Bennet's chastisement?

Bother. Before asking him, she should've

considered the possibility.

Cocking a lofty auburn brow at her, Lord Leventhorpe folded his ridiculously muscled arms across his Spanish-brown-encased chest. Slight disapproval gleamed in his blue eyes, more of deep slate at the moment. His mild, clean scent permeated the carriage's confines, which shrank with his hulking presence.

"Miss Culpepper, appearing in public before seven in the morning is not done. Especially with a lad younger than you— Oomph."

A particularly sharp turn sent him sliding his seat's length, and a giggle escaped her as she braced herself and Freddy to prevent the same.

Scooting to his corner, he anchored his shoulders firmly and stabbed a forefinger in the direction of the driver's seat. "Who, from the careening and uneven pace of this vehicle, has likely not driven a carriage. Ever. Not only is it unsafe, your behavior gives rise to gossip."

Bennet's inexperience explained the rocky ride to St. James Park and why she'd anticipated that last jostling corner. She'd blamed poor roads and worn springs. Warning Lord Leventhorpe would have been charitable, but his flailing about trying to retain his seat proved too amusing to forego. On the other hand,

Heath would not be pleased that someone inexperienced had handled the matched team and risked damaging an extremely costly conveyance.

"It's well beyond seven, my lord. Much closer to eight, I'd estimate." She didn't own a watch. "I cannot think it too terribly unfashionable, though somewhat unpopular, with sluggish souls reluctant to part with their mattresses before noon."

London's elite were a lazy lot.

Lord Leventhorpe's regard dropped to her grass-stained gown, disapproval fairly oozing from him.

Running in the garment hadn't been the wisest of decisions. She'd done enough laundry to know the delicate fabric was ruined. Regret chastised her at the shameful waste. Next time, she'd wear one of her well-worn gowns and pretend to be a servant. A borrowed maid's cap and cloak could be donned for good measure too. That shouldn't raise eyebrows or give rise to censure.

Grasping the seat as the carriage careened again, she caught a glimpse of her muddy half-boots. Her shoes had been sensible, though, and after a thorough cleaning would be no worse for wear.

"Blythe." His lordship's voice was low and affable, not condescending or judgmental. Something akin to concern tempered his deep baritone.

Chagrin pricked her. Perhaps she'd been off the mark, and he meant to be helpful.

He gestured at her gown. "I won't be specific as to why, but if the wrong person had seen your gown thus ... Well, they may have concluded you immoral or fast, and your reputation would have suffered greatly."

She gaped at him, something she'd done a great deal since arriving in London. "Because of grass stains? What in the world could be construed as immoral or fast about that?"

"Er, yes. Well ... it leads to speculation as to ... uh, that is, how they might have been acquired." He peered out the window and clawed at his lumpy neckcloth.

Oh. *Oh*!

Rot and bother. She sought the dirt-streaked floor, certain her cheeks had turned the same shade as her spencer and gown.

He'd used her given name. On purpose? Or had it been a slip of the tongue?

"I need to speak with Ravensdale about arranging riding lessons, in any event, and to inquire if your sisters or cousins wanted to venture to Tattersalls with us today." His mouth curved rakishly, and she caught a glimpse of the charismatic man of last evening.

Hmm. Perhaps he meant to take advantage of their

opportune encounter. Last evening he had said he'd call today. "My lord, forgive me if I overstep the bounds. Is it customary to call before breakfast?"

Lord Leventhorpe's wide grin creased the corners of his eyes. "Not at all. Raven's cook makes the most delicious crepes, and I crave them today. They aren't nearly as tasty at White's."

"She does, indeed. I've not eaten and confess I'm hungry myself." Blythe had been so intent upon conversing with Mr. Burlington last night, her food had gone almost untouched.

The carriage pitched, and she and Lord Leventhorpe clutched the sides. Good thing minimal traffic lined the streets. A blind hobgoblin possessed better driving skills than Bennet.

Righting his cane, Lord Leventhorpe settled into his corner once more. "Did you enjoy your first ball? The dancing? Your dinner with Burlington?"

His questions took her aback. Small talk, or was he genuinely interested?

"Yes, more than I expected to, truth to tell." Freddy laid his head in her lap and sighed. Activity outside the window suggested London had awakened fully in the past hour. "What do you know of Mr. Burlington?"

She couldn't ask Heath because he'd tell Brooke,

and then there'd be a bevy of questions launched Blythe's way. Why a man she'd newly met fascinated her, she wasn't ready to explain. Perhaps because he was the first to show genuine interest and not suggest an illicit relationship as had been the case when the Culpeppers had been pauper poor.

If Mr. Burlington's temperament mimicked his lordship's, stern and unapproachable, she wouldn't have been intrigued the least. Except she'd caught a glimpse of an entirely different man last evening, one Lord Leventhorpe seemed at pains to conceal.

Why? What tumult went on in that fiery head of his?

Drawing her attention from the street, she tucked another tendril of hair beneath her bonnet.

Lord Leventhorpe regarded her impassively.

Didn't he intend to answer? She'd probably broken a rule asking him about Mr. Burlington. Someone ought to write a book listing the ridiculous social expectations and decrees. They could call it the *Lady's Guide to Proper Comportment*, or some other such drivel.

He sliced a look outside before setting that disturbing azure-eyed gaze onto her. "He's a decent chap. Comes from good stock. No bad habits that I'm aware of." Lifting a shoulder slightly, he adjusted his glove. "Enjoys himself. Not a serious fellow, by any means."

He'd succinctly answered her question but hadn't told her anything, and his last words held a cautionary inflection. Perchance they weren't friends, or he didn't think it his place to discuss Mr. Burlington.

"You've a dab of dirt smearing your cheek, just there." Lord Leventhorpe indicated her cheek with a long finger.

Covered in dog hair, mud, and grass. Perfectly lovely.

Blythe wiped her face. "Did I get it?"

"No. You smeared the blob more." He chuckled and moved his fingers over his cheek, in imitation of where her smudge was. "You look rather like an adorable ragamuffin who's been making mud pies."

Blythe rubbed the spot again then examined her gloves. Earth marred the fingertips. Whether from wiping her face or from her tumbles in the park, she didn't know. Probably ruined her gloves too. "Better?"

"No. Allow me." He swiftly removed his black leather glove. "Lean my way a mite."

Blythe complied, and he bent and brushed his thumb along her cheek a couple of times.

Sensation darted outward, raising the flesh along her shoulders and arms.

The shards of silver in his gaze glittered as he stared into her eyes, and his touch lingered a fraction longer than entirely necessary. "You have the loveliest eyes and the most perfect mouth I've ever seen."

Such was the wonder in his voice, he almost seemed to speak to himself.

Blythe wet her lips, gone abruptly dry as autumn leaves.

His gaze riveted upon her mouth, tension tightened his lips.

He had the most beautifully sculpted mouth she'd ever noticed, and that included the Greek gods from last night's ball. Were Lord Leventhorpe's as warm and firm and tasty as they appeared?

What the blazes did Mr. Burlington's lips look like?

Did he have lips?

He must, of course.

A wheel sank into a hole with bone-jarring force, abruptly interrupting Blythe's mental rambling and pitching her and Lord Leventhorpe headfirst. His hat flew from his head as he tumbled from his seat onto his knees and reflexively wrapped his arms around her to keep her from plunging to the floor.

With a yelp of outraged surprise, Freddy bumped into Blythe's back, somehow managing to scramble onto the seat.

Their faces mere inches apart, Blythe couldn't haul her gaze from the glinting specks in Lord Leventhorpe's eyes. His focus sank to her lips, and his enlarged pupils revealed his arousal.

Would he kiss her?

Did she want him to?

Illogically, yes.

Breath suspended, she remained perfectly motionless. Waiting.

Lowering his head, he tightened his embrace an instant before his lips whispered across hers.

A brilliant light burst behind her eyes, and every bone in her body turned molten. She clutched his lapels, certain if she let go, she'd slither to the floor.

He ran his tongue along the seam of her lips, and, sighing, she readily capitulated and parted her mouth, eager to taste more of him.

They taste even better than they look.

The carriage jerked to an abrupt halt, and his head banged hers as they toppled to the floor, Lord Leventhorpe—Tristan—sprawled atop her and Freddy landing upon him.

The door sprang open almost immediately. "Where have you—"

Blythe craned her neck to peer beyond Tristan's

immense shoulder.

"Devil and damn." He swore beneath his breath before lifting his head and twisting to look behind him.

The entire household had awoken, and they'd trooped outdoors upon sighting the carriage.

"Good morning, Heath. Brooke. Girls." Stifling an absurd urge to laugh at their dumbfounded expressions, Blythe wiggled the fingers of her free hand in greeting. The other remained lodged between her and his lordship, trapped against his rigid abdomen. "We had a bumpy ride."

Blaire and Blaike burst into giggles.

Blythe didn't recall ever tittering that much at seventeen. She'd been the serious, sensible one. Except ... she'd giggled at Tristan mere moments ago.

"It must have been an extremely bumpy ride."

One of them snickered, but buried underneath his broad, delicious-smelling, *hard* body, Blythe wasn't sure which one. "Bennet hasn't much practice driving."

"Clearly." A glacier held more warmth than Heath's voice. "Do get off her, Leventhorpe. Your arse splayed upward atop my ward before I've even broken my fast rather annoys me and puts me off my food."

"I rather like it," Tristan whispered, his lips turned up devilishly as he waggled his eyebrows.

I do too.

Blythe gave him a playful shove. "Off before you cause a scandal."

He brushed her breast and hip as he untangled himself—surely unintentionally—yet hot, tiny pulses lingered where he'd touched her. After clambering from the carriage, Tristan righted his clothing, his expression gone unapproachable again.

Hmm, in public he was one man, in private another. Intriguing.

Heath assisted Blythe to the pavement. His brows swooped together upon noticing her soiled attire. The look he shot Tristan demanded an explanation. "We shall discuss this inside."

Replacing his hat, Tristan dipped his chestnut head in acknowledgement.

Heavens. Heath didn't think they ...? Heat suffused her. Utter hogwash.

"Wise, I think." Brooke cut her dark blue gaze to the sidewalk.

Nurses pushing prams and early morning-goers dotted the strip.

Curiosity glimmered in the twin's eyes as they grinned in unison. They'd barrage Blythe with questions the instant they cornered her alone.

"Blythe, you should mend your appearance before

anyone sees you." Heath looked to Bennet. "After you've seen to the horses and carriage, I wish to speak with you in my study."

Hat in his hands, Bennet shifted from foot to foot, apprehension furrowing his brow. "Yes, sir."

"Heath, please do not blame Bennet. I asked him to drive me." Blythe gave Bennet an encouraging smile. He mustn't lose his position because of her. "If anyone's at fault, it's me. I should have waited for the driver."

"You shouldn't have gone out alone at all, Blythe. This isn't Cheshire." Brooke stepped closer and lowering her voice, touched Blythe's arm. "You'll have to curb your impetuousness while in London. I know you're not happy here, and I'm sorry. Be that as it may, you cannot take off pell-mell whenever you've the urge. It isn't safe, and there are others to consider."

Blythe tamped her instinctive sharp retort. Brooke was right. Instead, she offered a falsely bright smile. "Of course, Brooke." Shoving her bonnet in place, Blythe searched for Freddy. There he was, already disappearing into the house. She angled toward the steps, eager to get off the street before passersby took notice of anything untoward. "I do hope breakfast is ready. I'm famished."

Thirty minutes later, everyone sat round the dining

table. Blythe had changed her gown and repaired her appearance, the whole while inundated by questions from Brooke and the others. Most likely, Tristan had endured the same interrogation from Heath.

Startling how a petal soft wisp of a kiss had her thinking of him as Tristan rather than Lord Leventhorpe. And she hadn't had a single thought of Mr. Burlington in the past hour.

Surely she hadn't already become as fickle and flighty as half of the women she'd met last night.

His plate heaped with crepes, Tristan took a drink of coffee. "Since I promised to call today to discuss riding lessons and our excursion to Tattersalls, I invited myself to join Miss Culpepper in her carriage." A boyish smile curved his mouth as he forked a piece of crepe. "And, I hoped to sample these."

Teacup halfway to his lips, Heath paused. "And you didn't give consideration to the impropriety of sharing a carriage alone with her?"

"We weren't alone. Freddy was there." Tristan popped the bite into his mouth and winked at the twins, who'd erupted into more giggles.

Blythe almost dropped the knife she'd been using to spread strawberry preserves. He'd made a jest. Who was this jovial stranger?

"All right, not my wisest decision. In my defense,

I think I spied Phillips at the park, and quite frankly, I had concerns about Blythe returning home alone." Tristan tapped his forefinger atop the lace tablecloth. "I suppose I might have followed in my landau. But I didn't, which I'll admit, may have provided the rumormongers fodder."

He'd done it again, used her first name, and no one as much as blinked. Perhaps because Tristan was such a close friend of Heath's, it was permissible. Or ... after the kiss, did he now think of her in more personal terms, as she did him?

"Heath, no one saw us. No harm's been done." She bit into her toast.

No one barring Mr. Maddox. And the drivers and passengers in the three—four?—carriages at the park. And anyone who'd glimpsed the inside of Heath's carriage as they passed. And those walking the street when they arrived home.

Botheration. A paper-thin line distinguished boldness from folly, and she may have inadvertently crossed it.

Two footmen and Jenkin entered, carrying enormous bouquets of flowers. "Ma'am, the drawing room can hold no more." Jenkin raised a spray of peach roses. "Where would you like these arrangements placed?"

Brooke's mouth curved. "Full? Already? I suppose the green salon then, Jenkin. Heath, have you room in the study? It's barely nine o'clock. I cannot imagine what the house will look like by noon."

"A confounded hothouse." Relaxing in his chair, he gave his head an amused shake. "I don't want to consider how many callers we'll have today." His lips twitching, he perused the dining room. "I may need to purchase a bigger house." Focusing upon each woman in turn, he rubbed his temple. "A *much* bigger house."

Tristan laughed, a melodious deep-throated rumble that teased her ears. The transformation from dour lord to amused rapscallion caused Blythe's heart to stutter oddly. Who was the real man? The affable chap who laughed easily or the caustic fellow? What had caused his prickly façade?

"Didn't you give that consideration before you launched this farce?" Undeterred by Heath's reproving scowl, Tristan indicated the women with a sweep of his hand. "What time will be convenient to take the ladies to Tattersalls?"

"Oh, I adore horses." Excitement lit Brette's eyes, and she leaned forward. "We're allowed to go, aren't we, Heath? I'm quite looking forward to our riding lessons too."

"As am I."

Blythe's fork clattered to her plate as she swung to the dining room's double doors.

Bearing an enormous variety of yellow flowers, Mr. Burlington—looking entirely too virile in a cinnamon-colored coat and beige pantaloons tucked into glossy Hessians, and wearing a confident smile—stood beside a disapproving Jenkin.

Mr. Burlington's God-like good looks drew the women's attention, aside from Brooke. She only ever had eyes for Heath.

They, like her and Tristan, had disliked each other upon first meeting.

Entirely different circumstances though.

"Sir. Madam. Mr. Burlington was most insistent he had urgent news to impart that could not wait until after breakfast, despite my urging that he wait in the drawing room, or better yet, return at a Christian hour."

Offering an apologetic quirk of his mouth—*his lips aren't as full as Tristan's*—Mr. Burlington patted Jenkin's shoulder. "I own, I exaggerated a mite about the importance of my visit. Surely desiring the company of these lovely ladies begs a degree of forgiveness?"

The majordomo's features puckered in further censure.

"Excuse me for calling unfashionably early." Holding the flowers, he approached the table, apparently intending to join them. "I wanted to make sure I was available to assist with the ladies, and Miss Culpepper assured me last night I'd be welcome, despite my forwardness."

His tawny gaze found Blythe and hovered upon her lips before skimming her bosoms.

The pair didn't offer as much as a tiny twitch this morning, and more incredibly, she detected not a jot of remorse for his brazen taradiddle.

He gave a flourishing bow. "These are for you, Miss Culpepper."

"Thank you. Yellow is my favorite color." Her gaze swerved to Tristan.

He regarded Mr. Burlington aloofly, though a hint of mockery tugged one umber brow upward. His gaze gravitated to hers, a question lurking in the ocean depths. Did he suspect Mr. Burlington lied?

"Won't you join us, Mr. Burlington?" Brooke indicated the chair beside Blythe as she bestowed a soothing smile on Jenkin. "Would you please see to a place for our unexpected guest?"

"At once, my lady."

"Oh, Jenkin, put these in water too, will you?" Mr. Burlington thrust the bouquet into Jenkin's arms. A lily brushed Jenkin's aquiline nose, depositing fine orange pollen over the tip, giving him the appearance of a giant duck. "I sincerely appreciate your gracious tolerance of my poor manners."

Jenkin's features softened the minutest amount. "I'll return with them in a few moments, sir."

If putting in an unacceptably early appearance was Mr. Burlington's singular fault, Blythe could forgive the *faux pas*, since she quite loathed tardiness. However, he'd fabricated that tidbit about her, which pricked rather sharply. She couldn't abide liars or contemptible treatment of servants.

After scooting his chair in, Mr. Burlington gazed round the table. "What time are we off to Tattersalls?"

Wickedness and scheming make one
unhappy, and a virtuous woman will avoid both.
~*Dignity and Decorum—The Genteel Lady's
Guide to Practical Living*

A week later, as the sun hovered between Hyde Park's horizon and the bright cloudless sky directly overhead, Tristan sat astride Buce, with Ravensdale and Burlington on either side atop their horses. No hint of a breeze teased the trees' lush foliage, and already the temperature promised to be quite warm.

A line of lissome blondes wearing stylish riding habits, each a different rainbow hue, and regally seated aside, negotiated a wide turn about Rotten Row and trotted to Francine.

She laughed, and after reining her horse round, clapped. "Splendid, ladies. You've quite got the knack of it. Well done."

"They're coming along nicely, aren't they? Francine has been a Godsend." Tristan shook his head. "I wouldn't have guessed she'd be such an apt teacher."

"They are enjoying themselves, which is what matters to me." Ravensdale rested an elbow atop his saddle. "They quite abhorred the notion of coming to London, if you recall. Blythe most particularly."

"Truly? I cannot imagine why. London is the epitome of culture, other than Paris, of course. I'd say Miss Culpepper is thriving here." Burlington's appreciative gaze remained fixed upon her.

Shows what you know.

Burlington moved forward a few paces. A newborn, blind kitten sucking a teat was less attached. Wholly besotted, he apparently didn't care who knew. He'd been impossible to deter, and not a day had passed without his company. A bit pompous and prone to embellishing the truth, he was still an amiable sort.

Tristan would have rather he concealed a vile, scandal-worthy secret, since it was difficult not to like the chap, and he'd been a dab hand at assisting with the lessons, even if he was barely short of a popinjay.

The men needn't have tagged along any longer, but none suggested they cease.

Tristan didn't want to stop, nor did he wish to

examine the reason why, though a befuddling suspicion jostled about in his mind.

"There are those who prefer the country's calm to London's chaos." *Including me.* "The Culpeppers were accustomed to a much quieter way of life on their dairy farm."

Why Tristan felt the need to explain, to defend Blythe, he didn't examine.

"Dairy farm?" That caught Burlington's attention. He tossed Ravensdale a surprised look. "They possess an estate? Most unusual for women. Do they own equal shares?"

"No." Raven spared Burlington a perfunctory glance. "Their cousin owns the farm. At least part of it. I won the rest from him and deeded it to my wife as a wedding gift."

Disappointment flooded Burlington's features. As a second son, it was no secret he needed to marry a woman with a heavy purse. Ravensdale had generously dowered Blythe, but still, given Burlington's lavish taste, that wouldn't last long—a year or two at best.

Which mattered more to the fop? Blythe or deep coffers?

Adjusting his position in the saddle, Tristan slapped his reins against his palm.

Blythe must be aware of Burlington's infatuation.

Did she return his regard? She wasn't a woman to display her emotions, willy-nilly, but kept them secreted. Her eyes hinted at her sentiments, but even an astute person would have to peer closely to see what lurked in their fascinating, periwinkle midst.

Since their kiss in the carriage—rather, since Tristan had stolen a taste of her utterly delicious lips, a kiss he could feel if he closed his eyes and pressed his lips together—she'd acted differently toward him. Her earlier hostility had been replaced by a watchful wariness and tentative cordiality, which seemed to increase as they saw each other daily, often more than once.

She'd granted him a waltz at each ball, something he looked forward to more than these morning rides. The pleasure of holding her tempting, svelte form made attending the nightly circuses almost bearable. He limited himself to a single dance, reluctant to have his thoughts coiled in her silvery tresses, or unable to rid her from his mind or dreams.

At least he no longer feared casting up his kippers or sweating through his shirt at public assemblies. More importantly, for the past three routes, he'd foregone his customary pre-appearance brandies.

What mystic power did she hold over him, that in a matter of weeks, he anticipated the future with renewed enthusiasm? He wanted to spend time with her, conversing, or strolling in serene silence. She wasn't one of those females who needed to fill the tranquility with senseless chatter.

When in her presence, his spirit found a peace wholly foreign to him; a vast contrast to the frequent and disturbing libidinous urges she also roused. Urges which accelerated to an uncomfortable level, sometimes requiring the discreet rearranging or concealment of his nether regions, easier done when not uncomfortably swollen like a Cumberland sausage.

"My lady will soon have to put aside her daily excursions." Ravensdale inched his horse near Tristan, saying in a low tone, "I'm going to be a father, Trist."

Tristan grinned, at once overjoyed for his friend and also experiencing a bewildering, envious pang. "Congratulations." He cut his gaze to Burlington, raptly gawping at Blythe. "I assume you're not making the joyous news public."

"Not yet." Ravensdale gave a short shake of his head then firmed his mouth, a shadow replacing the earlier joy in his eyes. "I heard you had an unfortunate encounter with Phillips yesterday afternoon."

"That's a marked understatement. I threatened to call the bastard out if he mentions the *incident* again." The churl had cornered Tristan as he left his lodgings, almost as if he'd been lying in wait. Retaliation for Tristan mangling his pretty face likely spurred Phillips's obsession. Or else he was an unconscionable bully who delighted in taunting others.

"Why such rubbish should matter to him after all these years, I cannot imagine. I think he finds perverse enjoyment in goading you." Raven waited until two young bucks rode by, animatedly discussing the bevvy of blondes they'd passed. Craning their necks for another glimpse, they collided and almost unseated the other, much to their snorting and prancing horses' displeasure.

Shaking his head, Raven grinned at their retreating forms. He dragged his focus to Tristan. "Because Phillips knows you still suffer the humiliation."

"Well, I refuse to hide my head or be ashamed any longer. I'm not proud of what happened, but I have come to accept I wasn't to blame. Hawksworth will be pleased. He's preached that particular, as well as forgiveness, countless times." Lifting a shoulder, Tristan twisted his mouth into a sardonic smile. "I suppose most adolescents would have been proud. You know that's not my way."

Raven quirked an eyebrow. "True. Monks boast more of their sexual exploits, and England doesn't harbor many monastics."

An exuberant, musical laugh floated across the green.

Blythe.

Wearing a robin's-egg-blue habit, she cantered her mare in a wide circle.

Like a bird to air, she'd taken to riding, and Tristan found himself awaking with renewed expectancy each morning, eagerly anticipating the lessons. No nightmares had plagued him either, despite running into Phillips at several functions and enduring his spiteful taunts. Only Rosemary Sanford annoyed him as much.

She continued to be a pushy, painful carbuncle. Now that Francine enjoyed the Culpeppers' company, Miss Sanford found her less malleable and less available. Unfortunately, that meant Miss Sanford had become tediously forward. Tristan feared she'd set her cap for him, and she had proven as tenacious as a hound tracking a scent. He could scarcely use the privy for fear she'd pop from the shrubberies or be waiting outside when he exited.

A pair of riders joined the women, and in a moment, the group headed to the waiting men.

Squinting, Tristan released a disgusted puff.

Phillips and Miss Sanford. Again.

Raven had finally conceded and introduced his

newly acquired family. Perhaps tomorrow's lesson would take place elsewhere since that pair had invited themselves three mornings in a row now, and after yesterday's ordeal, Tristan was done up with Phillips. His continued pursuit of Blythe proved worrisome too, particularly since Tristan had spied him in the park the day the cow wreaked havoc.

Miss Sanford, her seat excellent, galloped her horse ahead, clearly showing off.

Phillips remained with the others, but Lady Ravensdale maneuvered her docile mare, forcing him to the outside, away from her wards.

Undeniably ravishing in a black and plum habit, a breathless Miss Sanford ambled to a stop beside Tristan. "I bid you good day, my lords. Mr. Burlington. Isn't it a glorious morning? Why, I think we may have a delightfully warm summer this year."

In London, that meant stifling and putrid. All the more reason to return to Bristledale Court's fragrant meadows and fresh air.

"Good day, Miss Sanford." Scarcely glancing her way, Burlington bid her a distracted hello as Ravensdale and Tristan exchanged a brief look. Perhaps a proclamation would be forthcoming from him soon.

She wrinkled her nose peevishly at Burlington's

lackadaisical greeting.

"Pleasant day to you, Miss Sanford. Excuse me." Touching his hat, Ravensdale kicked his horse's sides and trotted to meet Lady Ravensdale. Likely to watch Phillips too.

"I'd hoped to see you at the Lockwood's soirée last evening." An invitation in her gaze and her lips bent coyly, Miss Sanford took the opportunity to sidle her horse near enough that their legs touched.

Buce dipped his massive head and snorted.

I agree, my friend.

Her cloying perfume assailed Tristan's nose, and he sneezed. "Beg your pardon."

Had she doused herself in the potion hoping to bewitch him? Or render him unconscious so she could have her way with him? Wouldn't do to gag and cough. Turning his head away, he gulped in a fresh breath. What he wouldn't give for a brisk breeze at the moment.

"I confess, I missed your company, my lord." A seductress's smile curved Miss Sanford's mouth, and the tip of her tongue darted out.

"I was otherwise engaged." And would be until naked cherubim, smoking cheroots, danced at Almack's. Her brazenness left him cold, and not a little worried for *his* virtue. He didn't trust her scheming wiles.

"Ho, Leventhorpe. Look who I ran into." Whitehouse and Maddox bore down on them, and Whitehouse half-saluted, half-waved. "Maddox has purchased a building near the docks, and I came upon him on my way here."

"Excellent to see you again, Maddox." Tristan took the opportunity to edge Buce away from Miss Sanford. "I'm glad you've decided to stay in England."

The other riders joined them. Introductions were made and greetings exchanged.

Scowling at Phillips, Burlington made for Blythe like a hawk swooping to claim its prey.

She nodded, a sweet smile stretching her kissable lips. The white feathers affixed to her hat's brim bounced as she responded to Burlington's comment.

Something he'd taken pains to make sure no one else heard.

The desire to push Burlington off his saddle onto his tight arse nipped at Tristan.

Lifting her head, the graceful arch of her swanlike neck stretched high to see above the crowd, she gifted Tristan with a stunning smile before veering her gaze to Francine.

He didn't doubt his huge grin made him look a lack-wit. She couldn't be that enamored with

Burlington if she smiled at him that way. Could she?

Burlington noticed the exchange, and a frown briefly tightened his features. He touched Blythe's arm, regaining her attention.

Well, perhaps he'd permit Burlington to stay in his seat. Poor love-sick swain.

You're not far off yourself, old chum.

Twaddle. Tristan wasn't the type to let feckless emotions run rampant.

Cheeks rosy, Francine fiddled with her reins and sent several covert peeks Maddox's way. She'd seemed quite taken with him when they'd met at tea last week.

Tristan heartily approved. Mayhap he could enlist Blythe's help in that regard. What a perfect excuse to call upon her. They could play matchmakers.

Maddox extracted his watch from his waistcoat, and after glimpsing the face, sighed. "I'm afraid I have an important appointment. I'm quite looking forward to dinner tonight, Lady Ravensdale."

"We have special entertainment planned." Lady Ravensdale slanted her head.

"Not special, I'm afraid." Blythe rubbed her mare's sleek neck. "I've been coerced into singing and playing the pianoforte."

"*Adequate* entertainment for a simple evening at

home, I'm sure." Miss Sanford's tone and falsely sweet smile indicated anything but.

"You haven't heard Blythe sing, Miss Sanford." Brette lifted her pert nose, a challenge in her tart response. "She's gifted."

"I'm rather anticipating her performance." Burlington turned to Blythe. "Perhaps you'd honor me with a duet?"

Burlington's puppy-like adoration caused Tristan's stomach to toss. Of course he sang. Probably had a ruddy brilliant voice too. Tristan's could be described as ordinary.

"Miss Simmons, dare I hope you will be in attendance?" Maddox's ears glinted scarlet in the early morning sun.

Blythe's gaze flew to Tristan's and, lips trembling, she wiggled her winged brows. Amusement frolicked in her eyes as she overtly slashed her gaze between Maddox and Francine.

Tristan swallowed a snort of laughter as Francine turned radish red.

"Francine, I assumed you planned to join me this evening." Miss Sanford's mouth formed an unflattering pout. "We're attending the theater tonight. Might you also be, Lord Leventhorpe?"

"No, I've been extended an invitation to dine with

the Ravensdales, as has my cousin, and I'm sure I'll enjoy Miss Culpepper's musical performance far more than Othello." He smiled at Blythe. He loathed Shakespeare, an unpopular sentiment among the tragedy-loving upper ten thousand.

"How ... gallant of you." Miss Sanford jutted her chin, scraping her caustic gaze over Blythe and the other ladies. She formed her lips into such a brittle smile, her face threatened to shatter with the slightest bump. "Another time then, my lord." She swung her horse in the opposite direction. "Mr. Phillips, I must return home. Mama and I have a fitting this morning."

"An appointment you've suddenly recalled, I dare say." Phillips smirked at her stormy glare.

"I shall accompany you, if you don't mind. I needed a word with you, Phillips." With a flash of his white teeth, Burlington lifted Blythe's hand. "Until tonight. The hours apart will be unbearable."

To prevent his guffaw, Tristan set his jaw and studied the array of leaves overhead. Why, there must be a dozen different verdant shades.

"I bid you good day." Phillips lifted his hat, and after a final, lecherous ogling of the ladies, and stabbing Tristan a darkling glare, he followed Miss Sanford.

Mrs. Sanford ought to rein her daughter in.

Keeping company with gentlemen of Phillips's ilk, even if he was in line for a viscountcy, wasn't to Miss Sanford's benefit.

An almost indecipherable frown furrowed Blythe's forehead when Burlington left. Because she didn't want him to go, or because of whom he'd departed with?

Smoothing her features, she gave Tristan a saucy smile. "You promised me a Gunter's ice when I mastered trotting, and given this warmer weather, I would relish the treat."

"You did promise, Tristan. And she's quite accomplished already." Francine shared a smile with Blythe.

Tristan couldn't have been more pleased at the friendship developing between them.

"Gunter's will have to wait. We have fittings too. Gentlemen, if you'll excuse us." With a regal nod, Lady Ravensdale indicated the women should follow her. Everyone, including Ravensdale and Francine trailed behind her.

"We can discuss a time for your reward tonight, Blythe," Tristan said as she passed him.

"Excellent, my lord. By-the-by, I told Brooke I would sing if you joined me." Laughing naughtily, she tore after her family.

"I'll be damned." Whitehouse chuckled. "You're smitten, Leventhorpe."

"I'm no such thing. I've come to enjoy the company of Raven's new family, and I've found I can tolerate public gatherings far better when they are," *she is,* "nearby."

When he was a child, Mother had forbidden any female house servants due to Father's wandering eye and groping hands. Tristan had believed the lack, in addition to the traumatic loss of his virginity, had predisposed him against females.

The Culpeppers had infiltrated the barrier he'd erected, and while the wall remained, he didn't feel quite the need to protect himself or be constantly on guard. He rose in his saddle to turn and peer behind him. Blythe's splendidly rounded derrière tucked into her sidesaddle bounced softly, earning an appreciative smile from him. The soft mounds would fit nicely in his hands.

Hell. Whitehouse *might* be right.

Was right.

How, in such a confounded short time, had that happened? How had he made room in his bruised heart for her?

Fingering his glass of port, Tristan crossed his legs and relaxed into the gold and navy brocade settee. Blythe sat before the pianoforte, her long, slim fingers dancing atop the keyboard as she sang a lively duet with Burlington. To Tristan's sheer delight, Esherton's bawling calves carried a tune better than the chap.

Burlington hit a particularly discordant note— *make that the sheep and crows too*—and Tristan flinched, though he studiously controlled his features and stared at his glass lest he laugh aloud. No one appreciated being laughed at, but, by God, couldn't Burlington hear himself?

Did Lady Ravensdale fear the cut-crystal mantel lamps might shatter? Or perhaps the diamond-paned leaded glass windows? Daring to shift his attention from his tumbler's scarlet contents for a moment, Tristan inadvertently snagged Ravensdale's eye and the trembling of his friend's lips nearly undid him.

Raven struggled as mightily as Tristan to curb his ill-timed humor. God help them if anyone dared snicker.

Blythe's beau wasn't perfect after all, and Tristan indulged in perverse, child-like satisfaction at the knowledge. Lifting his glass to take a sip, he hid his grin at the swiftly pained and masked expressions, determined and politely set mouths, and the occasional widened or startled eyes Burlington's inept performance produced.

God's toenails. Tone deaf as a flowerpot.

No. The comparison was unfair to the modest vessel.

Francine, more animated and prettier than Tristan had ever seen her, thanks to an extraordinary makeover by the Culpeppers, chatted quietly with an attentive Maddox. A union between the two would be a welcome blessing. Perchance the time had come to have a pointed discussion with Maddox and probe his intentions.

She deserved a decent man, and Tristan hadn't a qualm about Maddox. However, if he didn't have a serious interest in Francine, better to end things at once rather than break her fragile heart. Regardless, it was impossible to deny their absorption in one another. Both seemed oblivious of the camel caterwauling across the room.

Tristan scratched his nose, checking another troublesome sideways tug of his mouth.

Did camels caterwaul?

A silent petition to The Almighty followed lest he

lose control of his tenuous grasp.

Despite his unfortunate lack of talent, Burlington sang with gusto. Tristan had to give him credit for exuberance if naught else. Thankfully, Blythe's lovely voice penetrated Burlington's off-key, baritone warbling.

Brette hadn't exaggerated. Blythe was profoundly talented. Rather unfortunate that respectable ladies of station couldn't take to the stage or sing opera. Tristan didn't doubt she'd be tremendously successful—with a bloody mile-long line of suitors waiting to become her protector.

His earlier joviality fleeing, he pinched the bridge of his nose to ease the tension his scowl created. He'd cherished the unexpected truce that had sprung up between them. He deemed few women his friend, yet that description best fit the easy companionship they'd forged.

What you feel for her is markedly more than friendship.

A woman as striking as Blythe wouldn't remain long on the marriage mart, and the way Burlington diligently pursued her, Tristan had expected an offer by now. Why he hadn't made one perplexed more than a little.

Why Tristan minded confounded a great deal.

You know why.

He ought to forbid himself to ponder it. After all, *he* wasn't shopping for a marchioness. Yet. Still, he couldn't toss aside his disquiet like last month's gazette, which aggravated all the more.

Do shut up.

Blythe ended the piece with a flurry of notes, and everyone broke into applause and polite words of appreciation. Oblivious that the praise wasn't for him, Burlington beamed and nodded as if he'd made a stellar debut presentation and didn't budge from her side.

Blasted cheery ... tenacious ... grinning barnacle.

"Leventhorpe, I distinctly heard Miss Culpepper say she agreed to perform if you joined her." Whitehouse leaned a shoulder against the fireplace's Italian Bardiglio marble mantel, his mouth pulled into a slight smirk. "I don't believe I've had the pleasure of hearing you sing."

Pausing in her perusal of the sheet music, Blythe lifted her head, a silent plea in her gaze. "Yes, your lordship. I'd quite appreciate it."

Freddy's howling would've been preferred if it spared her Burlington's grating bellow in her ear as she'd endured the past three songs.

"I'm afraid I don't sing." Tristan took a hefty

swallow of wine. Not precisely true. He rather enjoyed singing and played the piano and violin too. Just not in front of an audience. True, the dinner had been intimate, and only a dozen people occupied the cozy, tastefully decorated drawing room, but he couldn't bear spectators.

Not since ...

"I understand." She bit her lower lip's outer corner, her shoulder slumping the tiniest bit. She flipped a couple more pages, hesitating briefly every now and again, before riffling through a few more. Probably trying to anticipate precisely how awful Burlington's contribution would be. "I'll find something suitable in a moment."

Suitable for a croaking bullfrog?

Blythe had graciously borne the evening's entertainment burden and had to have tired. Earlier, the women had harmonized to *The Joys of the Country*, and Drake, an accomplished pianist in his own right, had expertly played a Pleyel sonatina. Nevertheless, she'd played diligently for nearly an hour now.

"Heath tells me you have talent yourself, my lord." Lady Ravensdale looked up from the ... whatever it was she stitched—probably something for the babe given the tiny shape—and smiled at Tristan.

Bending his lips guiltily, Raven scratched his jaw.

"I might have mentioned it in passing."

Miss Blaike—or was it Miss Blaire?—clapped her hands. "Do humor us, my lord."

The pained look her twin slid Burlington said what no one dared.

For the sake of everyone's hearing and sanity, Tristan's resolve wavered.

"Please, Tristan," Francine implored sweetly. Desperately.

Ah, so she had been aware of the yowling.

"Oh, very well, if you agree to a game of loo afterward, Miss Culpepper." That relieved Blythe of further entertainment duties. Someone else would have to step in, or those present would have to find another activity to pass the time.

Please God, anything but charades.

"Bravo, Leventhorpe." Drake raised his glass in a mock salutation.

Tristan finished his wine and after setting the glass upon the marble-topped end table, blew out an extended, silent breath. *Get on with it, old m*an. He swung his foot to the floor. "I'm not accomplished by any means. Feel free to chat throughout, or cover your ears with your hands or pillows. I shan't be offended."

Could he ask them to look in the other direction too? Or remove themselves to another room?

131

"Your humility is admirable, my lord." A trifle reticent this evening, likely due to Hawksworth's surprising absence, Miss Brette rubbed Freddy's belly. "I'm sure your performance will be most pleasurable."

He gave her a gallant bow. "I shall endeavor not to disappoint."

Or break out into a cold sweat.

A grateful smile wreathed Blythe's face, and his stomach, or heart, or something in his torso, flopped uncomfortably.

He was almost certain the cause wasn't indigestion, nerves, or a fatal illness, though he didn't rule out poisoning. Phillips had been at the adjacent table at Brooks's when Tristan met Drake and Whitehouse there this afternoon. Fortunately, for once the cull had kept his mouth shut.

Through hooded eyes, Tristan indulged in a lingering appraisal.

God, Blythe was beautiful.

More than beautiful—exquisite—with her eyes glinting brightly in the candlelight, a slight flush of pleasure pinkening her cheeks, and her mouth berry red from nibbling her lips. A mouth formed for bewitching smiles and honeyed kisses.

Blythe had blossomed in recent weeks, and glowed from plenty to eat, enough rest, and happiness.

Her gown, a soft white with fine embroidered vines and purple flowers, the same vibrant shade as her eyes, hugged her ribs and emphasized the tempting flesh peeking above the neckline. Her skin couldn't possibly be as silky and soft as it appeared.

He'd never explore those rounded bits of loveliness.

Listen to him. Even his thoughts waxed poetic, and he didn't like poetry. Ridiculous, confusing, emotional drivel and rhyming poppycock written by infatuated, corkbrained ninnies.

"The vanquisher claims the plunder," Drake murmured, giving Tristan a devilish wink as he strode past *accidentally* kicking Drake's foot and earning him a wicked chuckle.

He was one to talk. That conversation wasn't fit for mixed company.

At the pianoforte, Tristan stood to the side, making it clear Burlington should move. "If you wouldn't mind? I need to stand there to read the music. My seat on the settee is available ..."

Burlington reluctantly conceded, but not before seizing Blythe's *ungloved* hand and ardently pressing his lips to the knuckles.

Bold, indeed, and outside the bounds. Tristan rather envied his audacity.

"Thank you for the duet." Her gaze narrowed almost imperceptibly as she extricated her hand and then smiled round the room before meeting Tristan's eyes. "Do you know *The Last Rose of Summer*?"

"I've heard it often enough, and I can read music." On the pretext of studying the music, he bent nearer. In truth, he wanted to sniff her perfume. She wore something different tonight, a light, musky scent with a hint of mint and vanilla? The glimpse of the lush valley between her breasts came as an unexpected treat. "You're wearing different perfume?"

She started, a half-smile bending her mouth. "Why, yes. It was an early birthday present from my sisters and cousins. They had a custom scent created for me. I'd been using a scent Heath gave Brooke since I had no perfume of my own."

"Might I sit rather than stand?" Giving in to impulse, he flipped his tails out of the way and eased onto the dainty bench's edge. Much less intimidating than standing and being the object of everyone's focused attention. Besides, Blythe sat closer to the others, and created a sort of human barrier.

Hiding behind a woman. How ungallant. He sneered inwardly. *Poltroon. Coward. Nidgit.*

"Of course." She scooted over, yet his rear hung halfway off the rectangular stool.

Claiming all but an inch, scarcely enough to be considered a respectable distance between them, he cleared his throat, now dry as parchment. This mightn't' have been a clever notion after all. A glass of anything cool would have been advisable given the more delectable view of her breasts as she bent forward to arrange the pages. His fingers twitched, yearning to explore the gentle slopes. The thin material of her gown did little to hide her long, slender legs, and the knowledge her bum rested so close to his caused an embarrassing rise in his trousers.

Think of something else.

"Your birthday is coming soon?"

"In ten days' time." Satisfied the pages were placed to read easily, she set her slender fingers to the keys. Veering him a sidelong look, she began the introduction. "The Wimpletons' have graciously agreed to host my birthday ball since Heath's house doesn't have a ballroom. You were sent an invitation."

Probably in the stack with his other unopened correspondences. He must hire a secretary. Or lease a house in Town and retain a butler. Dammit. He'd never entertained that idea before. What had beset him?

A whiff of perfume teased his nostrils and assaulted his senses.

Blythe had.

Dangerous entertaining such whimsical notions. No good could come of it. It was almost better when they'd been at constant odds. "And I most assuredly will be attending. Someone has to protect you ladies from the ne'er-do-wells."

"I'm sure Heath's counting on it. He's looking a trifle haggard these days." She chuckled, that throaty purr unique to her. "Miss Sanford too."

Tristan turned to her so swiftly, he almost lost his seat and grabbed the pianoforte's mahogany edge to keep his balance. He could use a nip of something. Anything. Tepid tea would do. He swallowed then gave a small cough. "Why do you say that?"

"I overheard her speaking, or venting, rather, to her mother at the modiste the other day. Quite by accident, I assure you." Coyness filled Blythe's indirect gaze, and a peculiar inflection shaded her tone. "I got the distinct impression she intends to be the next Marchioness of Leventhorpe. By Season's end."

With that unnerving disclosure, Blythe lifted her voice in song.

Tristan fell off the bench.

Of this one can be certain:
there is always someone with a mind
more devious and a scheme more sly than yours.
~Dignity and Decorum—The Genteel Lady's
Guide to Practical Living

8

A week later, sitting in Tristan's barouche, Blythe took in the bustle outside Gunter's Tea Shop. Given the number of carriages parked below the maples, many others had craved a cool ice on the warm day.

"What flavor do you recommend, my lord?" Patrons in the curricles beside Tristan's enjoyed an assortment of extravagant confections including a frozen berry-tinted treat and one that surely must be chocolate ice cream.

Though they'd operated a dairy farm, she hadn't tasted ice cream. None of the Culpeppers had ever indulged in anything extravagant or decadent. How did one choose from such an array of heavenly treats?

Tristan glanced up from his position beside his burgundy barouche's wheel. A few auburn curls dared to caress his beaver hat's rear brim. Attired in a cornflower blue jacket—an exact match to his eyes—black pantaloons emphasizing his long, muscular legs, tucked into slightly dusty Wellingtons, and a black and royal blue striped waistcoat encircling his torso, he cut a dashing figure.

Much too dashing for her to remain immune.

"I'm quite partial to the bergamot myself. It's a citrus similar to an orange. The barberry is also tasty." Tristan removed his gloves, and after acknowledging the greeting of a gentleman leaning against Berkeley Square's railing with a slight tilt of his head, laid the buff-toned leather on his equipage's edge. "I suggest you do the same, even if it's not the thing. When the ices melt, they can become quite messy. Your gloves are sure to become sticky and soiled."

"I'd like a barberry, please." Blythe drew off one glove. Wearing new cream kid-leather half boots, a soft green, almost white chintz overlaid with ivory lace and embellished with scalloped edges, and a brushed velvet eggshell-toned spencer, she resembled a giant gardenia. "Do you know what flavor you'd like, Blaike and Blaire?"

"Vanilla," they said in unison before bursting into giggles.

Of course they'd want the same flavor.

"Two vanillas, one barberry, and one bergamot." Tristan passed the young waiter a few coins.

"Yes, my lord." After another lingering look at the striking twins, the servant trotted across the square, dodging conveyances on his circumventive route.

Blythe might have accompanied Tristan to Gunter's alone without fear for her reputation— propriety allowed the excursion—but Brooke had deemed it wise to have the twins join them.

He hadn't objected to the extra company when he'd come to collect her and make good on Blythe's promised reward.

She had chaffed a mite at the forced chaperonage. After all, she'd been anticipating a precious hour or two alone with Tristan, and with the twins in tow, she'd be acting the part of governess. Though sweet, and not difficult of temperament, they possessed typical seventeen-year-old flightiness.

Mayhap not typical.

Blythe had never been featherbrained.

"Blythe, our friend Lady Claire is waving for us to join her and her grandmother. Might we?" Blaire indicated a cheerful redhead seated in a barouche farther along the square.

An elderly matron wearing a ghastly contraption teeming with ribbons and feathers atop her gray-peppered head smiled indulgently as Lady Claire, bouncing in her seat, waved and gesticulated enthusiastically at the twins.

"We can see you and his lordship. No one can suggest anything untoward." Blaike gathered her reticule and parasol, her gaze straying hopefully to her bubbly friend.

"I have no objection, but—" Blythe shook her finger as the twins leaped to their feet before she finished. "Mind your deportment."

Cause no scandal had been drilled into her these past weeks until she mumbled the phrase in her dreams.

Tristan assisted them to the pavement and chuckled as the grinning girls linked arms and hurried to their waiting friend.

"How do you tell them apart? They even have the same mole beside their left eyes." A slight crease lined Tristan's high forehead as he stared after them. "I have to memorize what they're wearing each time I see them, and that's after someone else addresses each, and I've deduced who is who."

Blythe laughed and shook her head. "If you spent

more time with them, you'd notice they have distinct features and characteristics. Blaire also has a mole below her right nostril. Blaike is more gregarious."

"Ah, good to know." He rested his elbows atop the barouche's side. "You seem to be enjoying London now."

A more youthful, relaxed man had replaced the stern one she'd met at Esherton. Removing her other glove, she slanted her head in contemplation. "I suppose so. More than I'd expected, honestly, and I've met a few charming people. I do loathe the constraints imposed on women here. I crave the outdoors, and I cannot even go for a walk by myself. The riding lessons have made my stay bearable."

As had his company. Once he'd stopped being a cross-as-a-bear boor. He and Heath were two of a few men who enjoyed and participated in intelligent conversations with her.

Tristan's expression grew pensive, and he cut her an indirect gaze.

Ah, the intriguing bashfulness again. What a paradox.

Almost as puzzling as why she went all soft and warm inside whenever he gazed at her like that.

"I have ..." He scratched his ear and cast his focus to the pavement.

A breeze caressed the maple leaves overhead, sending them cavorting and dancing to a soundless melody, their gentle rustling nature's harmony.

"This is the first Season I recall that I haven't been ready to depart for Bristledale Court upon a week of arriving in London."

Squinting, Blythe wiggled her toes in vexation. Guineas to goiters that was not what he'd been going to say at all.

Almost as if nervous, he drummed his square fingertips along the barouche's gleaming edge, his focus flitting here and there ... everywhere except on her.

"Oh? And why is that?" She'd pry the truth from his lips by one means or another. Blinking coyly and forming a moue in the same fashion she'd seen other wide-eyed misses gaze at their beaux, she almost choked on an inward snort.

Tristan stared at her as if she'd sprouted a disagreeable growth on her chin.

Her attempt at flirtation had fallen flatter than an oatcake. Seems neither she nor Tristan was adept at the art.

Now what?

Laying her gloves beside her atop the cherry-toned leather seat, she swept him a casual glance. And almost swallowed her tongue at the heat simmering in his azure eyes. Blue eyes ought to be cold, icy, yet molten lava tinged his irises.

Good heavens. Did he imply ...?

Surely he hadn't meant *she* was the reason. Had he?

Pleasant tremors tickled her spine and arms. What a stupendous, utterly wonderful notion. One that might alter her perception of London and her future dramatically.

His lips tilted almost shyly, and he clasped the carriage door in a white-knuckled grip. "I—"

"Here you are, sir. Miss." The servant passed Blythe a dainty cup brimming with pinkish deliciousness. He handed Tristan his then looked about in bewildered disappointment for a moment. "Where are the other misses?"

Another conquest for her sisters.

"They've joined Lady Claire." Blythe indicated the black and gold carriage. She wanted to dump her barberry ice atop his neatly parted hair for interrupting Tristan. Now she mightn't ever know what he'd intended to say.

"Yes, I see them." Tendrils of sweet vanilla dribbled down the glass's sides as the waiter scurried to the twins.

Blaike and Blaire had taken to London much better than she. Their enjoyment was genuine, hers a practiced pretense, made more bearable by Tristan's regular company. The girls seldom spoke of returning to Esherton ...well, the newly constructed house there. It wasn't quite finished. Brooke wanted to make the final decisions regarding the interior.

Did Blythe alone long to escape the city?

"Might I ask why you all have names that begin with a B?" Tristan winked and gave her a crooked grin. "It's rather unusual and a bit confusing."

Relaxing against the squab, Blythe raised a brow good-naturedly. "My mother and aunt wanted to continue a long family tradition. Every woman has been bestowed with a name beginning with the letter B. As you've no doubt discerned, Mother and Aunt Bess had to resort to some, ah, creativity. Poor Brette and Blaike have feminized male names. I don't think I'll bother with the custom when I marry. I already stutter and stumble saying our names half the time"

"Oh, I don't know. I'm partial to Brenna, Brownen, Brianna, and Byrony." He took a bite, and Blythe couldn't haul her gaze from his pursed lips.

How delicious a kiss would be from his slightly reddened mouth at this moment.

Tristan took another bite, closing his eyes and

making a contented sound.

God help her.

She scarcely checked the urge to lean forward and brush his lips with hers. Instead, she swallowed and attempted to gather her scattered thoughts. Spooning a taste of her ice, she savored the sweet coldness tingling on her tongue and cooling her overheated senses.

Grinning, he lifted his spoon. "You could expand the tradition to your sons. I rather like Bradford and Beauregard."

"Those are nice, I agree, and thus far, we've been spared a surname beginning with B. But gads. Can you imagine the confusion then?" Chuckling, she shook her head while enjoying another taste of her ice. "This is splendid, Tristan. Thank you."

"Blythe, I ..." A shadow darkened his face, and he shrugged. "I made you a promise, and I always keep my word."

Polite coolness had replaced the earlier velvety warmth of his tone, and she glanced at him sharply. In the past few seconds, something had changed drastically. His countenance grew aloof once more with the exception of a few stray sparks lingering in his gaze that he hadn't yet extinguished.

What the devil?

Taking another mouthful, she scoured her mind

for a reason for his abrupt transformation. How had talking about names beginning with B caused him to retreat behind his staunch comportment again?

Might as well see what he'd been about to say, even if it made her a forward hussy. She preferred candid speech to polite ambiguity or subtle intimations. "You were about to say something, my lord?"

His expression bland, he finally met her gaze straight on. Every hint of anything other than formal civility had vanished. "It was of no importance."

Dash it to Hades.

"If you're through, I have another appointment."

The nugget of hope that had had the audacity to raise its pathetic head shriveled in her chest and retreated to a safe cranny to bashfully hide once more.

Stupid heart.

Stupid him.

"That's the longest set, and possibly the most energetic cotillion, I've ever danced." Laughing and breathless, Blythe sank into a curtsy on the Wimpletons' ballroom floor. Her birthday ball was well-attended, a crush, truth to tell, and she'd been dancing nonstop for the better part of an hour.

Mr. Burlington, a fine sheen of sweat on his upper lip, bent above her hand. "Quite the most enjoyable one I've ever been privileged to share with someone as beautiful as yourself. Would you do me the honor of another set?"

A third? That wasn't done unless ... Did he intend to propose?

She pressed a hand firmly to her middle to ease her sudden collywobbles.

Anticipation or dread?

A month ago, she'd have predicted anticipation. Now ... Trepidation better described the peculiar sensation assaulting her middle.

Yes, wouldn't readily pass her lips. As clichéd as the phrase was, she needed more time. To get to know him better. Get to know Tristan better, especially after their outing to Gunter's Tea House. To decide whether she could abide Town life for more than this Season.

"I'm afraid the rest of my dances are already promised." She shouldn't have been relieved, and guilt kicked its petulant heels hard against her ribs. Wouldn't a woman desperately in love hurl convention aside to be with their sweetheart?

She would. But Blythe didn't love him.

"Ah, I should have anticipated that." Winking devilishly, he straightened and fished his kerchief from a pocket. "Next time I shall claim them all."

Acceptable if they were betrothed.

He dabbed his forehead, and after finishing, tucked the cloth away. Placing her hand into his crooked elbow, he guided her toward the terrace. "Would you walk with me outdoors for a spell? It's rather overwarm inside."

"A splendid idea." Unless he had another purpose for the suggestion.

Nonsense.

Even if he intended to propose, he wouldn't publicly. He'd been the embodiment of politesse these weeks past. She'd no reason to expect he would be otherwise tonight.

Besides, she feared her underarms were damp, such was the crowd, and her ball gown was an original. Hopefully, her perspiration wouldn't stain the fabric.

The Wimpletons, in collaboration with her dear cousins and sisters, had hosted an elaborate birthday ball in her honor. The house overran with yellow, peach, and white flower garlands and bouquets, as well as people wishing her well. She'd never had a grand birthday celebration, certainly nothing of this magnitude, and found herself overwhelmed and uncharacteristically emotional at the generosity and kindness.

A month ago, London and Society had rather appalled her, and now, the Season held more appeal than she'd ever foreseen. That didn't mean permanent residence in the malodorous city enticed. Visiting with the knowledge she'd be leaving and not returning was one thing. Staying on, enduring the continual scrutiny and rigid structures set by Society ... She shuddered slightly. And to think, some people thrived in this environ.

As Heath had predicted, the Culpeppers had niggled their way into *le beau monde's* good graces, after first rendering the *ton* off balance. Now they'd become wildly popular—as if she cared a beggar's purse about that sort of approval—and choosing what assemblies to attend had become a daily ordeal. A quiet evening at home had become a coveted thing of the past.

Such an abundance of flowers and sweetmeats arrived each morning, they'd started sending the previous day's tributes to local hospitals and orphanages.

The situation proved more amusing than flattering. Several gentlemen had called upon her, yet only two had captured her interest. Between Mr. Burlington's marked attention and having developed an unusual, yet comfortable, friendship with Tristan, deciding which gentlemen's company she preferred flummoxed her more than a little.

No. That was a fribble's nonsense.

Mr. Burlington's affections were as transparent as new glass. He constantly complimented her, and in recent days had hinted strongly of a future together, yet Lord Leventhorpe—the deucedly complicated enigma—continued to rouse her curiosity, and she feared, had engaged her heart.

One man was pleasant and predictable, like summer weather. The other, a discordant winter tempest. Given the choice between an easy-going, cheerful, good-natured god and a reticent, sometimes surly, impossible-to-figure-out man, the choice was obvious to a blind crone.

Only it wasn't. And that vexed her all the more.

Logic and reason clearly weighed in Mr. Burlington's favor, so other than patent foolhardiness, why did she prefer Tristan?

Yes, he had a splendid physique, and reliving their world-tilting kiss had kept her awake many nights, but muscles and a well-formed mouth weren't criteria for selecting a husband.

They could be. If he was the man.

Mr. Burlington hadn't approached Heath to ask for her hand—not that he had a say now that she'd reached her first and twentieth birthday—but, as surely as burning wood snapped and popped, a proposal would be forthcoming. She was as positive as Friday following Thursday it would be soon, too. Very soon. Perhaps tonight even.

She could be happy with Mr. Burlington, perhaps not blissful, but more than comfortable. Couldn't she? Everyone expected her to accept his proposal. Catching her lower lip between her teeth, she peeked at him through her lashes. He doted on her, rather in a smothering fashion at times, and seemed anxious to please. And he was gallant and strikingly handsome.

Why then, did something unidentifiable niggle at the recesses of her mind, enough to keep her from admitting to herself that her response to him was anything more than physical attraction? Maybe her lack of experience with men was to blame, although in recent weeks, she'd been exposed to all manner of males. Charming, witty, shy, awkward, arrogant, even a few who'd tried to steal a kiss and whose toes she'd tromped in response, or whose acquaintance she'd preferred to have been spared.

Mr. Phillips's taunting smile encroached upon her contemplations.

The last two balls, he'd attempted to maneuver her into isolated niches. No surprise that he'd identified each nook and cranny, every hidey-hole and dark corner in the grand homes they'd been invited into. Pests and vermin always found the best places to lurk.

Mr. Burlington patted her gloved hand as they approached the terrace. "I'll find you a seat, and then I'll fetch us something to drink. We can take our walk after we've had our beverages."

Ever the considerate gentleman.

A bead of sweat trickled between her breasts, and she unfurled her fan. Enthusiastically waving her fan, she welcomed the cooling breeze, insufficient as it was. "That sounds lovely. I'm fair parched."

"As am I." He smiled down at her, a sensual glint in his russet gaze.

After exiting the French windows, they paused for a moment beyond the threshold, and she inhaled the mild, blossom-scented air. Framed by flowering shrubs, roses, and an assortment of other blooms, the terrace would be stunning in the daylight. Lanterns, scattered here and there, lit the lawn and illuminated a quaint, fairy-like footpath. She yearned to explore the wending, moonlit trail through the manicured shrubberies.

They rounded the house's side, and Blythe smiled

in delight. A carved stone bench beckoned. It sat nestled between another pair of French windows and a pillar topped with a Grecian pot overflowing with flowers and greens. A faint light gleaming behind the partially drawn drapes revealed an unoccupied paneled library. No one milled this darker side, suiting Blythe fine. She relished a few moments of solitude, one of the things she'd craved most since leaving Esherton. "Perfect. I shall wait here."

Mr. Burlington lifted her hand, and after bestowing a fervent kiss upon the back, gently embraced her. His eyes darkened to jet-black shards, and his breath quickened.

He was going to kiss her.

She ought to object, yet her curiosity demanded satisfaction. Would his kiss be as devastating as Tristan's?

"Blythe." Mr. Burlington's mouth grazed hers, tentatively then more forcefully. He made a satisfied sound in his throat and sidled nearer, trailing his lips to her ear. "So beautiful."

Pleasant, though not world-tilting.

Blythe should've been disappointed, and yet she couldn't summon the false emotion.

"Please stop." She lightly shoved his shoulders. "Someone might come upon us."

A kiss in the garden wasn't likely to get her bundled off to the country, was it?

Breathing harshly, he released her. "I'm sorry. I've no excuse except that I was overcome by your beauty and the romantic setting. I've wanted to kiss you since the first moment I saw you." He flashed a boyish smile. "Please forgive my forwardness. I've been desperate to ask you—"

A laughing couple ran off the corner steps, likely seeking privacy as well. From what she'd glimpsed, the elegant garden provided several ideal locations for clandestine trysts.

"I should have stopped you sooner, but I confess to being curious." No sense pretending maidenly shyness. She'd wanted to know, and now she did.

His tawny brows peaked, and his lips curved into a gratified smile. "You were? And ...?"

Jiggling her closed fan at him, she laughed and sank onto the bench. "A lady never kisses and tells." Particularly if the kiss had merely been adequate.

Unlike Tristan's pulse-skipping, thought-scrambling assault on her senses.

"Please fetch our beverages, and then we can take a pleasant stroll." Perusing the tidy yard and neat flower beds, she pointed her fan at the flagstone walkway. "I'd like to explore that charming path. Do you know where it leads? "

"No, I've not had the occasion to wander it." His gaze skimmed the garden, the corners of his mouth tilting downward. "Are you certain you wish to remain here alone?"

Blythe relaxed against the seat's granite back. "I'm not alone. More than a score of people are a few feet away. I need simply call for assistance should I require it."

She could wrestle a calf or a sheep to the ground, so escaping a beau's unwanted attentions, should the need arrive, didn't concern her overly much.

"True. I'll return shortly." Mr. Burlington nodded slowly, before his face brightened, and he strode away, a perfect combination of male grace and refined breeding.

You could do far, far worse, Blythe.

She closed her eyes, and breathed in the perfumed air. Somewhere in the garden, honeysuckle bloomed.

The air escaped her in a frustrated puff.

Marrying into the upper crust hadn't been part of her plans when Heath towed them to London. She'd assumed she'd marry a simple man with simple ways and simple wants. Mr. Burlington, though not titled, came from a distinguished family and was accustomed to a privileged life. More on point, he adored living in

London, relished the hubbub, the assemblies, the noise.

How would he support a family? Her dowry would only go so far, and she'd eat her slippers before she'd accept another groat from Heath. Perhaps Mr. Burlington possessed his own wealth or had an income or allowance from another source.

She couldn't ask him though, now could she?

No, but she could ask Heath.

Blythe didn't mind hard work, and economizing was second nature. They could live modestly ... Well, she could. Could Courtland?—Mr. Burlington? She wasn't ready to call him by his given name yet which revealed much.

What about love?

Her eyes shut, she waved her hand before her nose, chasing away a persistent insect.

Perhaps her pleasant feelings toward Mr. Burlington would grow into something more. It was feasible. Why, a few short weeks ago, she couldn't abide Tristan.

He hadn't indicated interest beyond friendship, and he still kept a part of himself reserved ... almost as if he concealed a great secret or objectionable characteristic.

For a few moments that day at Gunter's she'd ventured to think he held her in esteem, until he'd donned his impenetrable mask again. She'd love to get beyond his exterior and have a glimpse of the real man. For the umpteenth time, Blythe tried to analyze her fascination.

"What is it about you, Tristan?"

"I cannot imagine why you whisper of one man when you've scandalously kissed another." Miss Sanford's haughty sneer nearly sent Blythe toppling off the bench in much the same way Tristan had tumbled onto his bum the other night.

Blythe bolted upright, her eyes popping open. "I cannot imagine why *you* think it your concern."

The chit had seen the kiss and wouldn't keep her painted lips sealed. Blythe peered beyond Miss Sanford's rigid posture. Had anyone else seen?

A dark figure, arms crossed, rested his shoulder against the house's corner.

Phillips.

Double Hades and purgatory.

Those two spent far too much time skulking about together for a couple not engaged romantically. Most peculiar given Miss Sanford's determination to leg-shackle poor Tristan.

Miss Sanford tromped to the bench's end, all pretense of civility gone. She placed her fists against her ivory and turquoise silk-clad hips and glowered.

157

"Did Mr. Burlington propose?"

Of all the unadulterated gall.

Blythe made a pretense of smoothing her already wrinkle-free satin skirt embroidered with gold spangles before half-spreading her French painted brisé fan. The impulse to verbally flay Rosemary Sanford overwhelmed her, and she had to lock her teeth and take a pair of deep, calming breaths. Apparently, Mr. Phillips and Miss Sanford had been close enough to see the kiss, but not hear her conversation with Courtland.

"Well. Did he?" Miss Sanford stamped her foot.

Petulant child.

Blythe could have sworn no one had been nearby when she'd arrived on this side of the terrace. What had Phillips and Miss Sanford been doing? Lurking in the greenery? Something was off with those two.

Blythe offered a noncommittal smile and ran her fingertips along the fan's lace edge. "I can't imagine why you think it your affair."

Her face contorted with loathing, Miss Sanford bent near Blythe. "It is my business if you intend to continue to throw yourself at Lord Leventhorpe. He's mine, you ... you country ... *neep*."

"Neep? Calling me a turnip's the best you can do?" Blythe stood five feet, ten inches tall. Did the diminutive nit think she intimidated her? She shoved Miss Sanford aside as she rose

Phillips stiffened and slowly eased upright, yet made no move to intervene.

Weasel.

Blythe elevated her chin, drawing her spine to its full extension. God, how she wanted to slap the termagant's hoity-toity face. "I have a word of advice for you, and if you've an ounce of common sense in your spiteful, conceited, prettily-styled head, you'll listen."

"I'm sure you've no advice I'd ever consider taking." Miss Sanford swallowed audibly and flung Phillips a hasty glance. "Why don't you and your hick sisters take yourselves back to the country where hobgoblin scarecrows like you belong?"

"Two of those *scarecrows* are my cousins, including *Lady* Ravensdale." Blythe unfolded her fan fully and made a pretense of drawing a finger down the delicate ribs to the handle. "We used to kill our own chickens. Do you know how?" She spared Miss Sanford a fleeting glance. Blythe hadn't killed a fowl, but she'd seen it done many times. Farm girls didn't have time for squeamish stomachs.

Miss Sanford clasped her throat, her eyes round as twin British crowns. "I'm sure I don't—"

"Like this." With a twist and a jerk, Blythe snapped her fan's handle, the crack echoing eerily loudly in the terrace's isolated corner.

Miss Sanford's jaw dropped as she took a stumbling step backward with a strangled shriek. "Mr. Phillips!"

Phillips remained alert, yet disregarded her plea.

What did she think? He'd suddenly become gallant? What exactly was their relationship?

"You'd better disabuse yourself of notions where Lord Leventhorpe is concerned. A few days ago, he told me succinctly that, 'cows will produce whisky before I'd ever marry Rosemary Sanford.'" Blythe's jubilant smile held no warmth. "His words, not mine, dear."

"That's a foul lie!" Miss Sanford released an infuriated gasp and swung her arm.

Blythe seized her palm in mid-air.

"I *shall* hit you back, and I promise you, your nose won't be the same." Blythe jerked her head toward Phillips. "Do you wish to look like him? Or worse?"

"You ... you trollop. Why am I not surprised you'd resort to such violent measures?" Miss Sanford yanked her hand free. "I'm going to tell Mama."

Tattling toddler.

"Please do. And be sure to explain why you are

prowling around unchaperoned with Mr. Phillips and how you tried to strike me first." Blythe tossed her broken fan onto the bench. "Consider carefully who my cousin-in-law is and who's in Lord Ravensdale's inner circle before you make an enemy of him. You mightn't find a single peer or respectable man willing to court you."

"Ooh. Ooh!" Miss Sanford fisted her hands and growled—*really growled*: a frustrated, infuriated suppressed roar—before turning on her heel and stomping across the terrace. She pushed Phillips hard in passing, and he laughed.

"Miss Sanford, I told you not to cross that vixen." Lust laced his sinister chuckle.

Where was Mr. Burlington? Shouldn't he have returned with her ratafia by now?

Well, Blythe wasn't dimwitted enough to loiter here with Mr. Phillips nearby. She might have the scandal she had wished for weeks ago, and now she wasn't quite ready to quit London.

She gathered her ruined fan—more wanton waste. When would she learn to control her temper?

"Miss Sanford is accustomed to having her way." Phillips meandered toward her, his bearing alert and predatory.

Botheration. Blythe had rid herself of one menace,

merely to be confronted by another.

She rounded the bench, intent on gaining the stairs leading to the yard. Unfortunately, that meant moving farther away from those assembled along the veranda and circumnavigating the shrubberies, which completely concealed her from view until she made the patio's other side.

"No need to scurry away. I simply want to ask you a question." He angled across the stones to the other set of stairs.

Blast.

He would cut her off, and finding herself cornered by that cawker spelled ruination. Heath had candidly warned them of Phillips's propensity to deflower innocents.

Waiting until he reached the top riser, she whirled and bolted toward the French doors.

"Dammit." Phillips sprinted after her. "Wait."

Blythe's hem tripped her, but she managed to regain her balance. The ruffled border ripped when she tore it loose. The gown could be repaired. Her reputation couldn't. She must make the library.

The slight hesitation gave Phillips the fraction he needed to reach her. He snaked an arm around her waist, and before she could twist free, crushed her to his chest. Chuckling lecherously, he panted against her neck.

"Let go, you oaf." Blythe reared away as she brought her knee up, jabbing his groin and shoving his chest with all her strength. The instant his grip loosened, she sprang free.

Cursing, he grabbed his crotch and doubled over. He tottered away a couple of steps, hunched like a hundred-year-old crone. "You'll pay for that, bitch."

She seized her skirts, and after hauling them to her knees, kicked him in the arse, sending him into the bushes below. "Touch me again, and I'll see you castrated faster than snipping a baby bull."

Shaking, more from fury than fear, she sprinted to the French doors.

Empty, thank God.

Panting, she eased the door open and slipping inside, took care to slide the lock home, even though Phillips wouldn't follow her any time soon. She needed a few moments to compose herself, and then she'd go in search of Heath and tell him what Phillips had attempted.

Dash it all. She couldn't.

As certain as sheep grow wool, he'd challenge Phillips. She pressed a hand to her forehead. The annoying ache that she'd attributed to nerves and excitement thrummed full on now.

Truthfully, she wanted to find Tristan and fall into his arms and ask him to break Phillips's nose again. Break a lot more than his nose. She summoned a wry grin. She'd become bloodthirsty of late.

She drew one side of the drapes closed and had grasped the second panel to do the same, when upset voices penetrated the door.

Blythe froze mid-movement.

"She tried to hit me, Mama. If I hadn't dodged her, she'd have broken my nose as she threatened to do."

Lying virago.

"Shh, Rosemary, hush. Here, step inside, and I'll tell you what must be done. That Culpepper chit will not hinder our well-laid plans. You *will* be Lady Leventhorpe."

The devil she will.

The door handle dipped.

Blythe dove behind the drawn drape. Drat, her toes stuck out, and she could be seen from outside. Under cover of the velvet and obscured by an oriental screen, she dashed to the corner beside the window. Cowardice didn't compel her concealment. Quite frankly, she wanted to know what those conniving women planned.

Tristan must be warned of their scheming.

Ears straining, she held her breath as the door swished open followed by the soft clacking of two pairs of heels.

"Rosemary, we must up our strategy immediately." The door clicked shut. "The Season is almost at an end. We'll arrange for you to be found in a compromising situation with Lord Leventhorpe. Tonight."

One who acts with integrity and
love will always be Victorious over
another's calculating and conniving schemes.
*~Dignity and Decorum—The Genteel Lady's
Guide to Practical Living*

9

Where was Blythe?

Ridiculous, this need to know her whereabouts. Or how much pleasure he drew from simply watching her ... listening to her.

Sipping champagne, Tristan stretched his neck and perused the colorful crowd swirling about the floor. The mirrored walls made the teeming room appear more crowded. Resting a shoulder against a Grecian column, he examined the ballroom and what he could see of the veranda, card room, and entrance from his strategic position.

Nothing.

She hadn't returned after exiting with Burlington,

though he'd re-entered several minutes ago and chatted with that American heiress, Margaret Hemple.

Why had he left Blythe outside?

Perhaps he hadn't, and she'd come inside by way of another door. The house did boast three other entrances from the garden.

Should he go in search of her?

He flexed his jaw.

She might not appreciate his interference or the knowledge that he supervised her whereabouts.

Mrs. Hemple laughed and stepped closer to Burlington, placing her hand on his arm and fluttering her eyelashes.

He murmured something while delivering one of his charming smiles, and her upturned face pinkened. Bending nearer, he covered her hand in a proprietary manner as he whispered in her ear.

Brows faintly scrunched, she flung a fleeting glance at the doors and slowly nodded.

After another brilliant smile, and pressing an indecently long kiss to her hand, he finally made his way outdoors once more.

Frowning a touch, Tristan took another sip of the sparkling wine and combed the room. *Again*. Fourth time in as many minutes. *Hopeless sot*.

He'd seen Burlington and Mrs. Hemple driving together in Hyde Park two days ago, and three days

prior to that, he'd come upon them at Gunter's. Thank
God it hadn't been the same day he'd treated the
Culpeppers to ices.

Did Blythe know her beau's devotion had strayed
or at the least was divided?

Should Tristan tell her? More on point, would she
care? Would Burlington's perfidy devastate her?

He derived no satisfaction from having at last
discovered Burlington's flaw.

Blythe seemed quite entranced with him, and if
the cur meant to toss her over for a wealthy widow,
better it happened now. Damnation. Too blasted bad he
couldn't blacken Burlington's eye if he did. Pursuing
her and engaging her affections if he didn't mean to act
honorably was outside the bounds.

To be fair, Mrs. Hemple had only arrived in
London a fortnight ago, and Tristan's subtle
questioning of Ravensdale and the Culpepper misses
revealed that Burlington still sent Blythe bouquets
daily and called as frequently. In recent days, he'd
accompanied the Culpeppers to several gatherings as
well. He couldn't have progressed to anything more
than a flirtation with Mrs. Hemple, could he?

Did he mean to court two women simultaneously?

Blythe needed to know about Burlington's
duplicity, yet Tristan didn't want to be the one to crush
her heart. He cherished their amiable truce, and hurting

her would be twisting a jagged, rusty knife in his chest too.

If Burlington wasn't trustworthy during courtship, would he stray after marriage?

Undoubtedly. Men of that ilk inevitably did.

Tristan stifled a yawn, rubbing the bridge of his nose with two fingers.

He hadn't been sleeping well again lately, except nightmares weren't the cause. Each time he dozed off, a vivacious, silver-haired, lilac-eyed, laughing nymph cavorted across his drowsy mind, jarring him awake. He couldn't quiet his mind or musings *or primal urges* when it came to Blythe.

Now he had a fresh concern regarding her.

She was going to get hurt. It couldn't be helped. Either she was told now or, far worse, she'd learn of Burlington's treachery later.

It wasn't his business, Tristan reminded himself for the umpteenth time. Fat good that did. His conscience and desire guffawed in unison.

If it hadn't been for his promise to Raven, and how seriously Tristan took his position in the House of Lords, he would've been tempted to make for Bristledale Court straightaway. He had no right entertaining fanciful musings about his closest friend's ward when Tristan wasn't looking to wed yet. That was why, other than a single snatched kiss, Tristan had steadfastly kept his acquaintance with Blythe a casual friendship, nothing more.

Except, the bond was much more. At least to him. Fate recklessly trod a path of destruction over his well-laid plans and laid siege to his heart.

He canvassed the room again.

No sign of her, or Phillips and Miss Sanford, blister it. They'd disappeared outside also, after exchanging a brief word with Burlington when he'd returned without Blythe.

Pathetic, Tristan knowing those trivialities. Everything regarding Blythe interested—*fascinated*—him. Attending these deuced functions didn't intimidate nearly as much with her present. Even if he wouldn't claim more than one dance, and his gut churned constantly with disquiet wondering if Burlington would propose, and she'd accept.

Particularly since Burlington's eye had strayed in recent days.

Perhaps his excursions with Mrs. Hemple meant nothing, and he intended to offer for Blythe, which made him an unconscionable knave for encouraging Mrs. Hemple's hopes.

A betrothal would put an end to Tristan's friendship with Blythe. No man approved of his wife keeping company with bachelors. He'd miss their witty conversations and her delightful, throaty laugh. No other woman compared to her.

If Burlington made her happy and content, Tristan wished them well. Who was he to reveal Burlington's perfidy? Perhaps Blythe didn't want to know. She wouldn't be the first woman to turn a blind eye to her husband's indiscretions.

Tristan couldn't offer her anything until he'd abolished his demons, and a sweetmeat tossed amongst starving urchins would last longer than Blythe on the marriage mart. She sensibly preferred Burlington's amiable personality, and Tristan knew full well others regarded him as unapproachable fellow.

He *had* been reserved prior to meeting Blythe. He hadn't smiled or laughed as much before becoming acquainted with the charming, strong-willed, vexing, sharp-tongued, wholly enchanting vixen.

Whitehouse had the right of it.

Tristan was smitten, and there wasn't a hell-fired thing he could do about it.

Still, caring for Blythe's wellbeing at assemblies was the least he could do for her and Ravensdale. Raven could scarcely watch all the moon-eyed swains and cocksure-blades swarming the other Culpeppers. One less woman to fret about would ease his mind and Tristan's.

He snorted softly.

God, listening to his vacillating, mental claptrap

made him want to slap himself. With a cudgel.

Phillips's persistent interest in Blythe proved disconcerting.

Hence at social functions, Tristan spent half his time following the unsavory cull, and the other half evading Miss Sanford's dogged pursuit. Why didn't the two leave off when the objects of their attentions didn't return their regard? Hadn't she or Phillips a morsel of pride? Or could they be so self-absorbed that they disregarded the other party's feelings? Not a healthy mindset and one that would certainly result in disappointment.

If it hadn't meant he would've had to enter into the parson's mousetrap, he would've claimed a secret betrothal to rid himself of Miss Sanford.

"Looking your usual pensive self tonight, I see Leventhorpe. Must be really enjoying *this* ball. I think it one of the better assemblies this Season, personally." Hawksworth's lopsided grin belied his sarcastic comment. Squinting, he scrutinized the ballroom's far side. "What the deuce have you been glaring at by the French windows the past fifteen minutes or more?"

"I see you finally escaped your parish." Tristan spared him a sideways glance. "How'd you manage that?"

Hawksworth chuckled, pulling his earlobe. "My official duties brought me to this side of Town, and

Drake cordially invited me to accompany him." He cocked his head, quirking a brow. "And don't think you can avoid answering the question by distracting me. You've downed two flutes of champagne, danced not at all, and the darkling scowls you've directed at Burlington and the benign beveled panes there," he jerked his head indicating the room's other end, "have more than one tongue wagging."

Tristan wasn't about to tell Hawksworth. "I'm contemplating whether I can make my escape."

Outside, to find Blythe.

Hawksworth shrugged and looked over his shoulder. "With this throng, I don't think our hosts would notice. There's hardly room to mill about. Smashing success." His keen gaze bored into Tristan. "How are you managing? You look all-in."

"Fine, as long as I keep my senses dulled." He paused in raising his empty glass when Phillips stomped past, a leaf poking from the hair above his ear, a smudge, suspiciously resembling dirt, along his knee, and ire smoldering in his eyes.

Blythe. If Phillips touched her...

Phillips made straight for Miss Sanford as she whispered to her mother and grandmother, all three staring pointedly in Tristan's direction.

That trio of Medusas couldn't be conspiring

anything good.

Thrusting his glass at Hawksworth, Tristan swiveled toward the French windows. "See if you can discover what Phillips has been up to. He looks like he's been frolicking in the shrubberies. Be discreet."

Jaw set and gut knotted, Tristan strode to the exit, dodging dancers and earning more than one vexed pout and scowl of displeasure.

Phillips's rumpled appearance, and his reputation for forcing women, as well as Blythe's continued absence, wreaked havoc upon Tristan's usually stoic conduct.

A glowing Francine and beaming Maddox intercepted him at the threshold.

Bloody he—

Tristan barely prevented the oath tapping irately at his teeth.

"Just the person we've been searching for." Francine fairly bubbled, her eyes sparkling and her cheeks rosy. "I ..." She gave Maddox an adoring gaze and nestled nearer him. "We wanted you to be the first to know."

"Am I to assume felicitations are in order?" Nothing of interest on the terrace beyond them caught Tristan's attention; therefore, he momentarily put aside his worry and offered a congratulatory smile.

Maddox's mouth lifted at one side as he slipped Francine's hand into his elbow's crook. "I hope you aren't offended I didn't approach you first, Leventhorpe. We were strolling the gardens, and I couldn't wait another moment to ask Miss Simmons, Francine, to become my wife."

"Not offended at all. I'm delighted." Tristan shook Maddox's hand and then pressed a quick kiss to Francine's forehead while surreptitiously scouring what he could see of the veranda and lawn. "My sincerest happy wishes to you both."

Dammit, where is Blythe?

"We want to marry straightaway, as soon as the banns have been read." Francine laid her hand on Tristan's forearm. "Tristan, would you give me away?"

A surge of emotion rendered him speechless. He swallowed and cleared his throat. "I would consider it a tremendous honor."

"Splendid. Come, darling, let's share our joyous news." Maddox led her away, and a crowd of well-wishers promptly gathered about them, though Miss Sanford wasn't amongst them.

Francine and Maddox made a brilliant couple and they were smitten with one another. Tristan found their devotion charming and truly touching. Perhaps his pessimistic nature had softened.

A trifle more light-hearted than he had been mere minutes before, he turned onto the veranda. A quick sweep of its length confirmed Blythe's absence. Hands braced at his hips and jaw tense, he turned one way then the other.

Which should he search first?

The garden, the pathway, or the veranda's other side? What about the lane to the mews beyond the fence?

He scratched his nape. Come to think of it, he hadn't seen a single Culpepper, or Raven, for that matter, for a good while. Not that he'd have noticed, intent as he'd been on seeking Blythe.

Besotted. Thoroughly and entirely. And doomed to disappointment.

"There you are, my lord. I worried you meant to stand me up for my dance." Lady Ravensdale glided his way, a vision in cream and lavender, a mischievous smile brightening her lovely face. "Although, I suspect you'd prefer my cousin to partner you."

She knows?

Tristan managed to keep his jaw from unhinging and crashing into his chest.

Winking, she swept nearer. "Your secret is safe with me, Lord Leventhorpe."

"I wouldn't be so inconsiderate as to miss our

dance, my lady." Actually, he'd completely forgotten the commitment. He wasn't about to address her second statement. If the day ever came that he admitted to what she insinuated, it wouldn't be in public.

"I'd offer to let Blythe dance in my stead, but I don't believe I've seen her since her set with Mr. Burlington. She's quite in demand tonight. It is her birthday celebration, after all."

Had the inflection in her voice altered the merest bit when she said Burlington's name?

Placing her hand upon his extended arm, Lady Ravensdale accompanied him inside. The blast of heat and body odors of a hundred people crowded into the insufficient space assailed him.

"Perhaps she's in the retiring room having a lie down." Lady Ravensdale smiled at a group of matrons chatting in hushed tones to one side of the windows. "She was feeling peaked earlier."

"She's unwell?" Had something happened with Phillips or Burlington to cause her malaise? Tristan could barely restrain himself from bolting upstairs and asking.

"No, nothing of that nature. She claimed a slight headache from the excitement. I advised her to take a powder and lie down with a cold cloth upon her forehead." Giving him a sympathetic smile, she curtsied prettily as the strains of a waltz filled the air. "I've sent her sisters to check on her and expect her to join us shortly."

"I'm relieved to hear it. I grew concerned when she didn't return after venturing outdoors with Burlington." Why didn't he blather a little more—go ahead and confess his infatuation?

"My lord, it's not my place to tell you, and I abhor gossip ..." Lady Ravensdale bit her bottom lip, and cast a guarded look about as he guided her past other swaying couples. "I overheard Mrs. Hemple a short while ago, quite inadvertently, I assure you." Her lavender-blue eyes so like Blythe's, Lady Ravensdale raised her pained gaze to his.

"What has you distressed, my lady?"

"Mr. Burlington has asked to pay his address to Mrs. Hemple, which must mean he has decided she would make a suitable bride. I'm afraid Blythe will be made a laughingstock."

Tristan missed a step, but quickly recovered and swung his head to the gaping French windows. Then why the hell had Burlington gone outdoors? To deliver the unpleasant news to Blythe? "Please forgive me, Lady Ravensdale. Are you certain? Burlington seems most devoted to Miss Culpepper."

She nodded, the curls framing her face pirouetting at her exuberance. "Oh, yes. I was in the retiring room suffering from a bout of nausea. They weren't aware I was behind the screen, and I was too discomfited and disturbed by Mrs. Hemple's announcement to make my presence known afterward." A blush tinted her face. "Mrs. Hemple confided her 'joyous news' to Lady Wimpleton. I think they are distant cousins, but I may have that wrong. I have no reason to believe she lied. I do want Heath to speak with Mr. Burlington before I tell Blythe in case I heard incorrectly."

Tristan would bet Buce she hadn't.

God rot Burlington, the unscrupulous knave. Tristan maneuvered Lady Ravensdale round Mrs. Sanford and her portly partner.

Miss Sanford's mother summoned a brittle smile and tilted her head before dragging her partner, huffing and puffing and sweating like a lathered horse, off the dance floor.

Had she overheard?

She'd practically followed Lady Ravensdale and Tristan as they'd danced at the expense of Mrs. Sanford's rotund partner who appeared about to expire from exertion. A naked doxy delivering a sermon from Hawksworth's pulpit claimed more subtlety than the eavesdropping Mrs. Sanford.

Damn. Tristan needed to find Blythe and tell her before that she-cat or her gloating daughter did. "Raven told me your wonderful news, my lady. Congratulations."

"We are very happy." A glorious smiled wreathed Lady Ravensdale's delicate features.

Their dance ended, and they went through the perfunctory bow and curtsy. Her eyes clouded when she gazed past him.

"Botheration. Heath has heard as well, I'll wager." Lady Ravensdale waved shortly at Miss Brette standing beside Ravensdale, a troubled expression tugging his black brows together. "My lord, I know it's not my place, nor yours, and I don't wish to impose or make you uncomfortable. But if you care for Blythe as much as I suspect you do, perhaps you can help ease her mortification and salvage her pride a degree?"

Given the wry twist of her lips, Tristan's astonishment must have reflected upon his face. "How so? We've established a truce of sorts, but Miss Culpepper is not exactly fond of me."

His heart twinged as he spoke, and she laid her hand on his forearm.

"You're wrong in that regard, my lord. Very wrong."

A man consumed with love or
lust schemes more than countless criminals,
and a diligent woman guards herself against his ploys.
~Dignity and Decorum—The Genteel Lady's
Guide to Practical Living

B lythe waited several interminable seconds after the library door clacked shut before daring to move. Tristan must be warned of Miss Sanford's intent to entrap him. Blythe ought to have exploded from behind the curtains and stopped the ill-hatched plotting, and had she not been utterly flabbergasted, she'd have corralled her wits sooner and done so.

Now she understood her instinctive dislike of Miss Sanford from almost the first moment she'd met her. The pert hussy possessed a warped soul.

She'd not sink her sorceress's talons into Tristan if Blythe could help it.

Edging along the drapery, she finally reached the

door. She fumbled with the blasted lock until it slid loose then whipped the door open. After a quick glance about the room and veranda, she slipped outside. No sooner had she shut the door then Mr. Burlington strode across the veranda, his eyes crinkled at the corners in excitement.

"Please forgive my tardiness." He drew his golden brows together a degree and sliced a swift glance behind her into the library. "I was detained. I hope you didn't become impatient, darling."

Darling?

Surely that meant he intended to propose.

Not now.

She didn't have the time to gently turn him down, for refuse his offer she must. He didn't stir anywhere near the kind of intense emotions or turmoil Tristan did, and those few minutes in the library overhearing Miss Sanford's wicked intentions had compelled Blythe to face what she'd denied for weeks now.

Stupidly, and against her better judgment, she'd gone and fallen in love with crotchety, obstinate, impossible Tristan. Her perverse heart had chosen the one man she could never have.

Love had an irregular sense of humor.

Casting about for a reason to stall the inescapable, she waved at Mr. Burlington's empty hands. "Where are our drinks?"

His cheerful expression faltered momentarily, and he gave a contrite laugh. "Eager to return to you, I forgot them."

What had he been doing then? He'd been gone upward of fifteen minutes.

He took her hands and gave her a sensual smile, calculated to soothe her ruffled feathers, she'd wager.

"You know I adore you, don't you, Blythe?" Advancing a pace, he cupped her upper arms, and brushed his thumbs back and forth, his eyes darkening to mahogany. "You captured my heart from the first moment I saw you. I knew you were refreshingly different from the coy misses. You're singularly unique. Special."

A bit overdone, there.

"Mr. Burlington ... Courtland ..."

"I want to marry you, dearest heart, I do—"

"I know you do, and I am honored—"

"But," he dipped his golden head as if intending to kiss her again, "I'm sure you also understand why I cannot ask you to be my wife."

Blythe leaned away and squinted at him. "You cannot?"

He continued to give her that roguish smile, the one that had set her heart aflutter and her bosoms puckering the first night she'd met him.

Nothing fluttered or puckered or gave the tiniest twitch.

"Cannot?" she croaked again. A dim-witted parrot sounded more intelligent. Blythe almost stuck a finger in her ear or shook her head to make sure she'd heard him correctly.

He had said, *cannot*, hadn't he?

And he expected her to understand why?

He seemed nonplussed for a flash.

Kicking her tangled emotions to next year, she narrowed her eyes further and examined every plane and angle of his handsome face, scrutinizing his countenance objectively for the first time.

How had she missed the slightly petulant turn to his mouth or the shrewd glint in his arresting eyes these past weeks? Those characteristics had been there, surely? Naiveté couldn't be blamed entirely. Truth to tell, she'd not wanted to see past his attractiveness and his apparent devotion. He *had* been courting her. She was neither slow-witted or given to fanciful imaginations.

Icy tendrils slithered round her shoulders and arms as she eased from his embrace. Shivering, she hugged herself. No honorable man called a woman darling when announcing he couldn't offer her marriage. What was his game?

"Please humor me and explain why we cannot marry." This should prove highly enlightening.

Courtland recovered his composure, or rather summoned his most engaging air, and closed the distance between them. Touching her cheek with his forefinger, he trailed it to her ear. "Surely you understand these things. My brother is not well. I'll likely inherit the title, and though I'm sure your dowry is quite adequate for a commoner ..."

Blythe slapped his hand away. What she yearned to do was plant him a facer. Right in his too-perfectly-straight, noble cork.

"Are you saying I'm not rich enough for you to marry, Courtland, or is it my lack of position that's objectionable? Or perchance both? I'm not wealthy *or* highborn?"

He blinked stupidly, as if surprised by her reaction. "Sweeting, don't take on so. No need to kick up a dust. I didn't expect to love the woman I take to wife."

How forward thinking of you. Dolt.

Tapping her chin, he delivered another of his disarming smiles.

Instead of his touch sending giddy ripples along her nerves, she fought the urge to cast up her accounts upon his gleaming shoes. She wrapped her arms tighter about her shoulders and drew her chin away.

He cradled her cheek in his palm. "You hold my affection, darling. I do love you, more than I believed I'd ever love a woman, and I am determined for us to be together. And I know you love me too. I've seen it in your eyes and the way you smile at me. You haven't been the least coy or reserved. Why, it's apparent, even to others. Several have congratulated me on my good fortune."

Had she been that humiliatingly obvious?

Stupid, stupid, *stupid* green girl.

"Although we cannot wed, Blythe, I have contrived a way for us to be together."

Did he not see the visual daggers she was hurling at him or the tense line of her mouth as she battled to subdue the curses she'd overheard in Esherton's barns?

His arrogant confidence raised her ire another notch. Fine then. Sent it hurtling heavenward, screeching in livid umbrage. "Do tell, Courtland. You've clearly thought this through. I'm most anxious to hear what you have *contrived*."

He nodded a mite too eagerly, and she curled her toes and fingers tightly to maintain her composure. How would he like a nose like Phillips's? With precisely the right angle and enough force, she was certain she could manage something similar ...

"Such arrangements are not uncommon, and with a rich wife, I can indulge your every want." He brushed her cheekbone with his thumb.

"How ... generous of you."

"I know you were dreadfully impoverished in your prior life, and must covet the fineries you've been denied." He cast a hasty glance around and dared sidle a pair of paces closer. Indecently close, truth to tell. "I'll treat you far better than my wife, I assure you. I merely want her money, nothing else. She's simply an inconvenience I must endure." He skewed his mouth to the side. "Well, I'd have to beget an heir. Perhaps a spare as well to assure the title continues."

Why stop at two? Try for a half dozen.

Blythe went rigid and dropped her clenched hands to her sides as her stomach pitched to her shoes. Pasting a falsely sweet smile upon her face, and carefully modulating her tone, she unfurled her fingers. Better to scratch his deceiving, conniving, treacherous ... blackguard eyes out. Good God. What had she ever seen in this conceited, self-centered lout?

"Are you suggesting..." She sucked in a slow, steadying breath.

Lord, help me not to attack him.

Cocking her head, she forced the foul words past

her tongue. "Are you offering me carte-blanche? You're suggesting I become your mistress?"

She pressed a hand to her roiling middle. Pity women couldn't fight in affairs of honor. She'd call the ruddy cur out, except she neither knew how to brandish a sword nor fire a pistol. Heath did, and would challenge Burlington in a blink if she told him about the affront. With a babe on the way, that bloody well wasn't going to happen.

"Yes." Courtland grinned excitedly, moving forward and compelling her to retreat until she bumped into the pillar beside the doorway. "It's the flawless solution—"

Flawless? No.

"—don't you agree?"

Agree? When cows poop gold.

"Phillips suggested the brilliant remedy. We can be together, sweeting, and I can do my duty to my title and family." He reached for her again, but she evaded him, fervently looking about for something to clobber him with in lieu of a club.

How could a man be so dense? Thick as oak and ignorant as a rock. Did he think she'd grasp the chance? That the honor of becoming his paramour held such appeal she'd toss her reputation and her family's into the gossips' cesspool?

Courtland winked conspiratorially and waggled his eyebrows. "I've already selected an heiress."

Poor woman, whoever she was.

"Oh. Is she someone I know?" The pillar shuddered, and the pot atop it rattled when Blythe—intent upon dodging Courtland's grasping hands—bumped into it.

Uneasiness creased the edge of his mouth, and he slowly shook his head. "I don't believe so. She's an American widow, and tonight, she agreed to allow me to court her."

Hence his tardy return. Did he expect Blythe to wish him joy?

He tipped his mouth into a boyish, almost bashful smile. "That's what delayed me. I'm sorry I wasn't forthright from the beginning. I worried you might take offense and react peevishly, but you're such a sensible woman—"

"How considerate of you." Tarring and feathering was too good for the likes of him. Nipping his ballocks off might be appropriate.

She dropped her broken fan, and he promptly bent to retrieve it.

Ever the gentleman.

She seized the potted plant, staggering from its surprising weight. She lowered her voice seductively.

"Courtland?"

"Yes, darling?" He glanced up, his brandy-colored eyes widening in shocked comprehension.

"I wouldn't be your *whore* if the king decreed it." She released the plant atop his head, smiling in satisfaction when he toppled like a foxed-to-the-gills tippler.

Happy birthday to me.

Two laughing couples swept up the steps, stumbling to a stop and bumping pell-mell into one another upon spying him. A startled yelp escaped a woman as she clutched her companion's arm.

With the exaggeration of someone who'd practiced the art repeatedly, the other lady pressed her hand to her bosom, shut her eyes, and swayed dramatically. "Is he ... dead?"

One could hope, but if so, the gibbet awaited Blythe. She'd likely only concussed Mr. Burlington though. A few more curious passersby peeked above the bushes before breaking into frenetic whispering.

One fellow raised his quizzing glass and peered through the lens, as if he needed help distinguishing a man's prone form splayed upon the pavers, dirt sprinkled upon his face, and a red geranium upright upon his forehead. "I say, what happened to Burlington?"

"I declined his proposal." He had made a proposition, all right. Just not an honorable one. "As you can see, he didn't take the refusal well. Keeled over straightaway."

With her assistance.

He moaned and moved his head slightly, earning him sympathetic murmurs from the quartet.

Blythe neatly stepped around him. She couldn't dredge up an ounce of remorse. "You might want to summon a physician."

Or don't. Let the bugger rot.

She'd ruined her chances of making a suitable match. Whether Burlington was a cur or not, plopping pottery atop aristocratic heads, especially gorgeous, eligible ones, didn't fly well with the upper ten thousand.

Just as well.

She'd allowed the pomp and flattering male attention to woo her, fool her into thinking Society wasn't horrid after all. People did, indeed, see what they wanted to see. Well, no more. Succumbing once to foolhardiness might be excused. Doing so again made her fair game and she deserved everything slung her way.

She inhaled deeply. Enough self-castigations for now.

No one knew better than she how gullible and susceptible she'd been. There would be plenty of time to dwell upon her foolishness and chide herself to purgatory and back. Right now, she must alert Tristan. It might be too late already.

Fearing what she'd eaten today was about to make a reappearance, Blythe lifted her skirts and bolted into the library. Stumbling over the threshold, she yelped in alarm when a hand clamped onto her arm.

Phillips.

And he wasn't alone. Miss Sanford also occupied the room. Vengeance glittered in their hardened gazes.

Why in blazes did Blythe keep encountering these miscreants? Did Fate simply have a rancorous streak?

"Unhand me!" She wrenched free of his grasp and spun to flee whence she'd come, except Phillips sprinted to the door ahead of her.

He smiled—equally gloating, arrogant, and merciless—and shoved it shut with an ominous thud. The lock slid home disconcertingly loudly, but the rasp of him dragging the curtains closed caused the hairs along her nape to lift.

Hopefully, Phillips slamming the door alerted the foursome outside. Would they notify anyone? They might think Blythe was simply having a fit of temper. Or were they too focused on Mr. Burlington to have noticed?

"Precisely the person we sought." Miss Sanford's expression settled into crafty lines, and half-seated upon the divan's gold and taupe damask rolled arm with her arms crossed, she slanted Mr. Phillips a sly glance. "So, Mr. Burlington threw you over, did he? Cannot say I blame him. Personally, I found it astonishing he'd deemed to wallow in muck."

"Tsk, tsk." Mr. Phillips stood with his arms akimbo, eyeing Blythe toe to top. "Serves you right, putting on airs. He's picked another mark, has he? Someone with a much flusher purse. His family might possess an old title, but they're pauper-poor, and he has to marry for money. Some of us have been blessedly spared that obligation."

Had Mr. Phillips and Miss Sanford been listening at the door? How else would they have known what had transpired between her and Mr. Burlington?

"I'll allow, I did rather admire his other clever notion." Leering at Blythe's bosoms, Phillips ran his tongue over his protruding bottom lip. "Wait. I suggested the idea."

Every part of Blythe tried to shrivel to escape his lewd appraisal. If only she had her shawl to shield her cringing flesh. She thrust her chin upward and marched to the interior door. They could bugger themselves before she rose to their bait. Miss Sanford's presence in the library gave Blythe hope she hadn't yet succeeded in cornering Tristan.

With an unladylike snarl, Miss Sanford leaped to her feet. Blocking Blythe's path, she jabbed a forefinger at her. "You're not going anywhere. I'm tired of you interfering. It's taken me the better part of two Seasons for Lord Leventhorpe to pay me any note."

Blythe released a snort worthy of a bull's admiration. "Vain imaginations from a chit too dull-witted to see the truth."

"You're not going to destroy what I've striven for. I won't be forced to marry that ancient, smelly, doddering fool my uncle has selected for me because he insists I gain a title." Flapping her hand, Miss Sanford sneered, her face contorted like a child in the midst of a tantrum. "Especially since Mr. Burlington has tossed you aside."

Her exultant smirk proved she relished Blythe's situation.

Find Tristan.

As Blythe sidestepped to go past, Phillips seized her from behind, trapping her with an arm below her breasts and his other pressed across her chest in a crushing embrace. "You're staying here with me, in order for Miss Sanford to snare herself a lord."

Not if Blythe wanted to keep her virtue, she wasn't.

From the satisfaction shining in their evil gazes, it didn't take a scholar to discern that was precisely what Phillips and Miss Sanford intended.

My total ruination.

He licked her ear, pressing his forearm into her breasts until she feared they'd breach her bodice.

Revulsion sluiced through her and sent her scalp puckering.

Stomping upon his foot with her heel—blast, what she wouldn't have given for her sturdy half-boots—she gulped in a huge breath, prepared to let loose with a banshee's screech meant to peel the paper from the walls, warp the coffee-and-emerald-toned marble encasing the fireplace, and bend the brass tools propped to one side.

Phillips anticipated her scream and slapped his sweaty, dirt-streaked palm over her mouth.

Writhing against him, she gagged and choked.

Chuckling, the sound gravelly and deranged, he dragged her, struggling and attempting to bite his hand, away from doorway. His sour odor sent another surge of burning bile to her throat. Blythe's lighter weight and his iron grip prevented her from wriggling free.

The key clasped in her gloved fingertips, Miss Sanford glided from the library with a triumphant smile and mocking wave.

Now how would Blythe warn Tristan?

An instant later, the lock turned.

The witch had locked Blythe in the library with Phillips. How could anyone be that calculatingly evil?

Miss Sanford had arranged for Phillips to despoil her because she mistakenly believed Blythe competed for Tristan's affections?

Nipping her neck hard, Phillips seized her embroidered muslin gown at the nape. His breath coming in ragged gasps, he ripped the fabric down her back, accidentally giving her the small amount of slack she needed to slip free.

His debauched laugh as she sprinted away toppled her stomach. Her neck throbbed where he'd bitten it though she didn't think he'd broken the skin. She didn't dare touch it to find out. She needed both hands to preserve her modesty.

"I hoped you'd be a fighter. They're the best to bed. Not the chits who whimper and beg for mercy. They concede too easily." The crazed glint in his eyes intensified. "I'll wager you'll fight until the end."

He's utterly mad.

She darted behind the settee, trying to keep her

breasts somewhat covered while searching for a weapon with one eye and keeping her other trained on Phillips.

Grinning evilly, he stalked forward. "No one knows you're in here except Rosemary, and I'm certain, for once, her lips are tightly sealed. Both doors are locked. You cannot escape me, Blythe."

God, please.

Blythe crept along the settee. She had one chance, and it meant baring her bosoms to Phillips's lascivious scrutiny. Scooting another few inches, she bit her bottom lip and deliberately let her bodice dip lower, revealing her insignificant *décolletage*.

He paused midstride, his gaze flicking to hers before gravitating to her breasts again. He licked his lips, his face gone taut with lust. "If I didn't know better, I'd think you were teasing me with your tits."

Disgusting, crude pig.

"You won't get away with this. Heath will kill you." Her gown slid to her elbow, the golden embroidery threads shimmering where the lamps atop the fireplace mantel cast their glow. She left the torn material where it gathered at her crook, the entire side of her breast visible.

His gaze remained riveted to her exposed flesh. Just the distraction she needed.

A few more inches.

Phillips was almost upon her.

She released her dress, and the lace-encrusted cloth bunched at her waist.

Jaw sagging, he gaped.

She seized the poker.

Understanding dawned, and head down, like an infuriated, thwarted bull, he lurched forward, blaring profanities.

Shrieking, she thrust the poker with all her might as he collided with her, slamming her head into the marble at the same instant the French window shattered and a madman's bellow filled the room.

Dropping the poker, she slumped to the floor, Phillips's weight crushing her, as something warm and sticky gushed down her face. She struggled, trying to call for help.

"Tris ... tan."

"Blythe, sweetheart." A moment before she slipped into the frothy black fog wreathing her head and senses, torment-filled ocean-blue eyes hovered above her.

God can't stand schemers; therefore, the poor
and rich alike fall into the pit they dig for others.
~*Dignity and Decorum—The Genteel Lady's
Guide to Practical Living*

11

"**B**lythe, darling? Can you hear me?"
Disregarding the crowd merging into the
study from both entrances, Tristan roughly shoved
Phillips off Blythe.

Phillips moaned, but didn't move.

Tristan didn't spare him a second glance as he
stripped off his coat then gently laid the cutaway upon
her chest and torso, providing her a modicum of
modesty.

Pulverizing an unconscious man was outside the
bounds, but, God help him, he ached to render Phillips
a beating he wouldn't recover from. Tristan gritted his
teeth against his rage. "Hell."

Blood oozed from a gash on the side of her head.

When he'd heard her scream and broke the door ...
He would kill Phillips if she hadn't already.

Pressing his handkerchief to the wound, he
attempted to staunch the blood's flow and shield her
from the curious onlookers. "Sweeting, wake up."

"Tristan? Miss Sanford ... don't trust ..." Moaning,
she opened her eyes briefly, her gaze black and
panicked, before they fluttered closed again, and she
fell insensate once more.

The library continued to fill with snoops and
gossips, and perhaps, a few truly concerned people.
Their voices rose and fell in undulating waves of
speculation, distress, and censure.

Without fail, the busybodies would take it upon
themselves to jump to conclusions and render a
judgment then eagerly pass the falsehoods along before
knowing what had actually happened.

The intruders' comments melded together in a
grating mélange.

"What happened?"

"Is she dishabille under his lordship's coat?

"Why is Phillips lying there?"

"Is he bleeding?"

A woman gasped. "He looks ... *dead*."

"Stuff and nonsense. His chest is rising and
falling," a man calmly advised.

"Oh dear, you don't suppose he ...?"

"Compromised her?"

"She does rather look set upon."

"What's Lord Leventhorpe about?"

"Whatever was Miss Culpepper doing alone with Phillips? Surely she knew better."

"Perhaps it was an arranged *tête-à-tête* that went too far."

Nothing of the sort. A coddled, scheming wench and a black-hearted whoremonger merely conspired to ruin an innocent.

The prattle droned on as guests tossed conjecture about like confetti at a wedding until Tristan bit the inside of his cheek to keep from shouting for the lot to bugger off.

Drake crouched beside Tristan and swore softly. He touched Tristan's shoulder, speaking low. "Whitehouse went to fetch her family and the Wimpletons. Hawksworth and I shall deal with Phillips."

"No. Leave him." Tristan met Drake's acutely troubled gaze, but refused to grant Phillips a glance. If the bloody arse weren't already dead, Tristan wasn't sure he wouldn't strangle him on the spot. He meant to reserve that pleasure for the field of honor.

A fireplace poker, the tip bloodied a good four

inches, lay beside Blythe. Her blow hadn't been a missish swat. She'd meant to impale Phillips, and had done a hell-fired job.

"Is he still alive?" Tristan ground the question out between clenched teeth. Maybe Phillips's earlier groan had been his last.

Drake gave a terse nod. "Regretfully."

"Will you act as my second?" Tristan took Blythe's cold hand in his. He was a useless nurse. His luncheon tried again to reappear, and he swallowed the burning scraping his throat. "Can't see Hawksworth in the role. Man of God and all, and I won't put Raven in that position."

"Aye. You mean to call Phillips out then." It wasn't a question.

"Better me than Ravensdale. He has a passel of women he's responsible for and a child on the way."

"Really? I'd not heard. Still, Miss Culpepper's not your responsibility." Drake shifted, glaring over his shoulder and gesturing away inquisitive guests venturing too near. He turned to Tristan. "Some will question your purpose."

Tristan sat on his heels, chin tucked to his chest and palms pressed to his thighs. He spoke discreetly. "She'll have to be married at once. You know that. The scandal will be monumental. Who better than me to wed her? I've spent a great deal of time with the family since their arrival in Town. If Raven can be convinced to claim Blythe has agreed to wed me, that gives me the right to demand satisfaction. Announcing our betrothal will validate her refusing Burlington, and we can spread it about that's why he set his sights on another."

Burlington wouldn't refute the falsehood. It might ruin his chances with his fresh conquest.

"Dear God, what has happened?" Lady Ravensdale and the Culpepper misses descended on Blythe like avenging angels, crowding around her and forcing Tristan to move aside. Face wan, Lady Ravensdale motioned to Ravensdale, thunderous rage sparking in his eyes and hardening the angles of his face. "Heath, please have Lord Wimpleton send for a physician at once. And someone, hand me that knitted throw on the armchair there."

Hawksworth swiftly complied, and in moment the blanket protected Blythe from prying eyes.

Damn, Tristan would have liked to call for the magistrate too. A waste of time, though. A peer would never see the inside of Newgate much less have his aristocratic neck draped with a noose. Phillips stood a better chance of mysteriously disappearing, something Tristan wasn't averse to. All the more reason to meet

Phillips upon the dueling field. Theirs would not be a match to first blood match. Someone should have dispatched Phillips long ago.

Tristan would meet with his solicitor in the morning and change his will. Better to err on wisdom's side and be prepared.

Would Phillips choose pistols or swords?

Pistols.

He was too cowardly to risk a test of blades.

Clasping his nape with one hand, and resting the other upon his hip, Tristan stood above the women surrounding Blythe, their pretty faces ravaged by angst and apprehension. He wasn't family, and he had no right to remain, excepting his impulsive intent to claim Blythe as his newly betrothed. But his feet, as if weighted with loadstones, refused to move.

Blythe remained motionless, her face ashen and her glorious hair, red-tinged on one side, spilling about her head.

If Whitehouse hadn't overheard the commotion between Blythe and Burlington and promptly sought Tristan ...

He'd almost been too late.

Scorching fury nearly choked him, the blazing heat setting his blood afire. He made an inarticulate sound, half growl and half oath, causing Miss Blaike—

or was she Miss Blaire?—to flick him a confused look. He hadn't experienced hatred this intense since ... No. Not even when he'd been victimized and publicly shamed.

His need to protect Blythe, now more than ever, diminished everything else.

"We need handkerchiefs." Brette thrust her dainty chin upward and extended her hand. "Now, if you please."

Several ladies and gentlemen obliged, including Hawksworth.

"Let's allow Miss Culpepper and her family some privacy, shall we?" Lady Wimpleton took charge and ushered the curious gawkers from the library. "We've supper to eat, and the musicians continue to play. Go along now. I shall keep you apprised of the situation, but Cook will have my skin if her preparations have been in vain. A footman will watch for the physician and deliver him here straightaway." Her gaze scooted to Phillips, and scorn twitched her lips. "I shall send a servant with linens, though I'm sure the carpet is beyond redemption."

With a sharp-eyed, telling glance at her husband, she followed their guests from the room.

Lord Leventhorpe looked askance at Phillips, making no effort to assist him. "Ravensdale, have you any idea what has transpired?"

Ravensdale nodded curtly as he veered his attention to the women. "I've a suspicion, but would prefer not to discuss it now."

"Just so. My thoughts as well. My support is yours, of course, in whatever manner you should need it." Wimpleton's attention fell upon the pillar lying beside a bookshelf. "I see you made good use of that wretched thing at last."

Tristan didn't dare look at where Hawksworth and Drake had dragged Phillips. If Blythe's blow hadn't knocked the bastard off his feet, Tristan would have leveled him.

He closed his eyes and clamped his teeth until they ached.

Rustling behind him drew his attention. Prodding with one foot, Whitehouse nudged Phillips in the side, none too gently. "Wake up, you piece of ..." He slung a shielded glance at the women hunkered around Blythe. "Odious lump of horse excrement."

Blaike raked Phillips with an infuriated glare. "That's much too polite a description for the likes of him. A barnful of ripe, maggoty cow manure is less offensive."

"Is there water to be had? Or spirits? I imagine a splash or two ought to revive this rabble." Whitehouse examined the room before poking Phillips harder. "What about smelling salts or a vinaigrette?"

The Culpeppers shook their blonde heads, and Brette said, "We don't faint, and I don't recall a single instance where we've needed salts.

How badly had Blythe speared Phillips? Brilliant on her part. She had to have been terrified. Another rush of wrath heated his blood. The dastard would use his injury as an excuse to avoid the duel, and Tristan had no intention of allowing Phillips to escape the repercussions of his actions this time.

Phillips cracked an eye open and weakly shoved at the tormenting shoe. "Leave off trying to crack my ribs, you bloo—"

"Stubble it." Whitehouse jabbed Phillips's side once more. "There are ladies present."

"Not all present are worthy of the title, I can assure you." Groaning, Phillips crawled to his knees, one hand clasping his crimson-stained lower abdomen. Curling his lower lip, he glowered and jerked his chin in Blythe's direction. "That one's a teasing wh—"

Whitehouse planted his foot on Phillips's chest, sending him flying onto his back.

"Damn you, Whitehouse." Phillips struggled into a sitting position, white-lipped and shaking.

Tristan was upon him in three strides. He hauled

Phillips to his feet, and tugged him within an inch of his nose, snarling into the sod's frightened face. "That's my betrothed you're maligning."

Phillips blanched and sputtered, his frantic gaze circling the room. "I ... I ... didn't know."

"What's he talking about, Heath?" Confusion riddled Lady Ravensdale's harried whisper.

A cunning edge replaced Phillips's unease. "It seems no one did. How very peculiar."

"You accosted and compromised the woman I've pledged to marry." Tristan had to swiftly establish his right to demand satisfaction, even if he lied like Zeus in the process. He'd worry about Blythe's reaction later. If she found marriage to him abhorrent, he would at least have protected her from dishonor by giving her his name and a marchioness title. He'd allow her to live where she chose and provide for her the rest of her days. Hell, he'd grant her a divorce, though they were harder to come by than King Solomon's treasures.

"Blythe's to marry Lord Leventhorpe?" one of the twins said. Impossible to tell which with his back to the women. "When did that occur? Why didn't anyone tell us?"

"I thought Mr. Burlington held her affections." The other twin?

Bad enough they looked exactly alike, but

identical voices too?

"A ruse, perhaps?" Brette hit the mark closer than Tristan liked.

Did she suspect he spoke out of turn?

"Or perhaps, there's no betrothal at all. I hadn't heard a word of it. Why would an affianced woman agree to meet me privately?" Phillips stood a mite straighter, confident in his smug arrogance.

Perchance Blythe had merely nicked him, more's the pity.

Tristan shook him, and Phillips winced, pressing his other hand to his groin.

"Surely she understood what such a clandestine arrangement with me entailed, and she chose ruin regardless."

The men's outraged exclamations mixed with the women's shocked gasps.

"Considering I have you in my grasp, you're an utter beef-wit to continue to besmirch her honor." Giving Phillips a mocking slap, Tristan permitted himself a gratified smirk and stepped away. "I demand satisfaction. Name your second."

"Leventhorpe, no. That's my place." Ravensdale's vehement protest was muffled by a ruckus in the corridor and Lady Ravensdale's quickly stifled cry of protest.

The door exploded open, banging into the shelving beside it and sending several volumes tumbling to the floor. Everyone's attention hurtled to entrance.

Miss Sanford plowed into the library, followed closely by her thin, stern-faced elderly uncle, the Earl of Marfontaine. She rapidly scanned the room, her focus alighting upon Blythe. "I told you, Uncle Rupert, she was in here with Mr. Phillips." Miss Sanford pointed a shaking finger at Blythe. "After rejecting his proposal, she clobbered poor Mr. Burlington and, wanting to be alone with Mr. Phillips, demanded I leave."

What was she about? Dragging her uncle in to witness Blythe's disgrace? Was this another attempt to discredit Blythe? Pathetic and contemptible.

"As I explained earlier, and as Miss Sanford has this instant confirmed, Miss Culpepper was more than willing to accept my advances." Keeping his distance from Tristan, and clutching his stomach, Phillips, pale and sweating, edged toward the door. "I tried to warn Burlington of her duplicity, but the man wouldn't listen."

"Stay right where you are, Phillips." Ravensdale shut the door in the face of goggle-eyed, eavesdroppers, preventing Phillips's escape.

No doubt several guests also stood beyond the

drawn drapes listening at the shattered French window. The pillar's convenient location had enabled Tristan to hastily break in. Otherwise ...

Sure enough, glass crunched and someone hurriedly shushed another lurker. Whitehouse tramped to the drapes and, notorious for his devilish glowers, stuck his dark head between the folds. The noise of scurrying footsteps and muted voices filtered through the heavy fabric.

"And stay away." Whitehouse took a position at the mangled window, acting as a deterrent if others dared to venture near enough to listen.

It didn't matter. The gossipmongers wouldn't stop talking about tonight for a decade.

A partially disrobed woman, bleeding from her temple, found alone in a library with a man skewered in the gut, and both lying upon the floor unconscious provided tattle simply too delicious not to bandy about. And Phillips's reputation as despoiler of innocents was the Devonshire cream atop the gossip's cocoa.

Triston shut his mind against the names people would be calling Blythe else he would finish Phillips now.

"I'll be going then." Phillips unsteadily sidled closer to the door.

"You've been challenged to an affair of honor.

And if my ward had been 'more than' willing, as you vulgarly claim, pray tell me why she's unconscious and you've been stuck with a poker? I don't believe you for an instant." Ravensdale crossed his arms and slid Tristan a sideways glance. "You will name your second before leaving, or I shall demand satisfaction as well."

"I tell you, no duel is necessary." Phillips waved a hand in an exaggerated gesture. "I pardon Leventhorpe for striking me. I understand he's in a dudgeon. There's no need for such extremes over a woman. She's not even highborn."

Every Culpepper's gaze pelted him with blue-violet darts.

Maybe Tristan would save them a great deal of trouble and run Phillips through with the poker now. He searched the room. Where had the tool gotten to?

Hawksworth, ankles crossed and one hip resting against the black walnut, leather-topped desk, rested one hand upon the brass length, a knowing gleam in his eye.

Knows me too hell-fired well.

"Did you hear me? I pardon you for striking me." Perspiration beaded Phillips's forehead and upper lip.

Caused by pain from his injury? More likely a coward's fear of looking down a pistol barrel.

"How magnanimous of you. I assuredly don't pardon you, especially since I can think of nothing more worthy of defending than the virtue of the woman who shall soon be my wife."

By God. I mean it too. I shall willingly forfeit my life for Blythe's honor.

Tristan must marry her before the duel, to assure she was provided for if Phillips proved lucky.

A rivulet of sweat trickled from Phillips's temple to his jaw. Fear, most assuredly. "Well, as for Miss Culpepper's injury, we became too rough in our play. I shall make my apologies when she is recovered."

"That's outside enough! I shan't permit another lascivious word spoken in the presence of my sister and cousins." Lady Ravensdale angled her chin proudly and decapitated Phillips with her affronted gaze. "Gentlemen do not discuss such uncouth matters in the presence of innocent young ladies."

"But Miss Sanford just proved I spoke the truth." Phillips sounded quite desperate. Men that preyed upon women and those weaker than themselves frequently revealed themselves limp-spined cravens when faced with equals or someone stronger.

Phillips cowered before Tristan's more formidable figure.

"Balderdash and poppycock. My lying niece

didn't validate your sorry tale, and she is not without fault in this." Marfontaine gave her a severe look. "Rosemary, I heard you conspiring with your mother."

He seized her elbow when she shook her head and opened her mouth to protest.

"Be quiet, chit. It took me threatening to cut your Mother off to finally pry the truth from her. As it is, she'll not get a groat for the next month." He sketched a brief bow to the Culpepper misses, his wiry fingers clamped Miss Sanford's arm. "Permit me to introduce myself. The Earl of Marfontaine. I humbly apologize for my niece's involvement in this bumblebroth. Rest assured, she will be dealt with severely."

"Uncle ..." She twisted her arm, trying to break free. "You don't understand."

"Enough." He gave her a slight shake. "I've already spoken to Lord Bexley. You will be married by special license the day after tomorrow."

"No. No! I'm sorry." Weeping noisily, she clawed at his hand. "Please, Uncle Rupert. Mr. Phillips forced me to help him. He threatened me, said he'd beat and despoil me or worse as he had dozens of other women if I didn't. If I helped him, and kept quiet about my involvement, he promised he'd make sure Lord Leventhorpe was made to marry me. He gave me his word."

The word of a scheming cur—worthless.

Miss Sanford had outed Phillips, made him an enemy, and Tristan almost felt a jot of sympathy for her. Good thing he intended to meet Phillips in two days' time, or he feared what might happen to her. Phillips possessed a violent, vengeful streak.

"Tell them, Mr. Phillips," she wailed. "You bragged about your conquests. Said you had at least a dozen by-blows."

More offended gasps and ire-laden noises escaped those present.

The wintry stare Phillips skewered Miss Sanford with caused Tristan's heart to trip. There was the ruthless villain Phillips took such pains to conceal. Evil shadowed his eyes before he veiled his hatred.

"That's utterly despicable." Lady Ravensdale presented her back, giving him the cut as Blythe stirred and put a hand to the side of her head.

Swinging to Tristan, Miss Sanford extended her free hand, fat tears leaving dual paths down her pale cheeks. "Please. I love you. I'll do anything. Don't let him make me marry that odious old man. He farts and belches constantly." She hiccupped and swiped at her wet face. "And he smells of cabbage and tobacco."

"You'll marry him, or I'll ship you off to a convent in France or Spain." Marfontaine's mouth bent a fraction, and he chuckled, the rasping drier than straw in August. "You like your luxuries far too much for that stark way of life, my dear."

"Miss Sanford, as I've tried to explain to you numerous times, I have never entertained any notion of courting or marrying you." Tristan cut Blythe a rapid glance.

She appeared to be rousing. Eyes open, she blinked in confusion.

"It's because of her, isn't it?" Thrusting her arm at Blythe, Miss Sanford laughed, a high-pitched cackle tinged with desperation or madness. "She's completely compromised. No one will have her now."

"I shall." Tristan's attention remained on Blythe.

Her unfocused eyes widened slightly, and her lips parted.

Marfontaine propelled Miss Sanford to the door. "Gel, if you don't leave off, I'll commit you to Bedlam instead of foisting you on poor Bexley. Might be better for him in any event. He'll likely cock up his toes within a year to escape your shrewish tongue."

Phillips waited until Marfontaine opened the door. "By-the-by, Miss Sanford ..."

She flung him a belligerent scowl, snapping, "What?"

A purely evil smile arced his mouth. "Leventhorpe

claims he and Miss Culpepper are trothed."

Phillips's gleeful announcement had the desired effect.

Miss Sanford collapsed into Marfontaine's arms, sobbing.

"But why would Lord Leventhorpe say he and Blythe are to be married if they aren't?" Brette addressed the question to no one in particular.

"We are."

The faint response had every eye in the room ricocheting to Blythe propped against Lady Ravensdale.

It can be plainly confessed of
the old and young, the wise and the
ignorant, and the rich and the poor, that despite
their best schemes, circumstances far more often
govern mankind, than man controls circumstances.
*~Dignity and Decorum—The Genteel Lady's
Guide to Practical Living*

12

"**L**ord Leventhorpe waits in the drawing room." Brooke tentatively touched Blythe's arm as she gazed out her upper story bedroom window. "You must see him. There's much to discuss and put to right about last night."

"Yes. I know." Blythe let the lace panel fall into place as she swiveled and smiled at Brooke. "Don't look pensive. Everything will work out." *How, I have no idea.* "The situation isn't a complete catastrophe." *Pretty dashed close, however.*

Groggy and muddled, Blythe had believed the

scene in the Wimpletons' library part of a wretched dream when she'd agreed to the betrothal. His desperation, or perhaps the emotion in the depths of his vivid blue gaze had been pleading. Nevertheless, it had silently called to her across the distance, drawing the response from her before she'd considered the consequences.

Once she'd regained her wits, there'd been plenty of time to consider the magnitude, and her foolish impulse, though propelled by compassion and a befuddled state of mind, had further complicated the impossible situation.

Uttering those two little, yet significant words, "We are," had been immensely satisfying. Miss Sanford's reaction to Blythe's verbal blow, even more so. Shame pricked her conscience. Deliberate unkindness wasn't a trait she normally exhibited.

What had possessed Tristan to declare they were betrothed?

Compassion? Pity?

She dared not hope he felt something more.

"I won't have you miserable or forced into a marriage." Brooke wrapped an arm around Blythe's waist. "Heath has spoken to Leventhorpe. He's sincere about his offer, and I suspect he cares for you. Leventhorpe isn't the scoundrel I'd first judged him to be." Her mouth hitched to one side. "Though he is quite the most aloof and unreadable man I've met."

"Not at all. That's a well-rehearsed protective front. Tristan is sensitive beneath his stern mask." Blythe scrunched her brow while fingering the silky turquoise tassel dangling from the curtain tie-back and observing a pair of mourning doves that had swooped onto an elder's branch, the lone tree in the tiny side garden. "I think he's been wounded, terribly hurt, somehow."

What had happened to create such a lasting scar and the hardened barrier he kept securely around himself?

An extended silence met her oral musing. She pried her attention away from the cuddling grayish-brown birds to find Brooke staring at her, head canted to the side and a speculative spark in her dark-lashed eyes.

"What's that look for?" After running her fingers through the silky strands one last time, Blythe dropped the tassel.

"You defended him and called him Tristan." A grin threatening, Brooke adopted a maternal mien instead. She twirled a curl near her ear. "Might I ask how long that has been going on?"

"An inadvertent slip of the tongue, I assure you.

But if he's to be my husband, I suppose I'd better become accustomed to it." Unless Blythe could convince him to cry off. Not likely, any more than he'd forgo that preposterous duel. The scandal wouldn't just tarnish her. The disgrace would affect the rest of the family, too, and possibly ruin Brette and the twins' chances of a decent match.

Plain ludicrous how Society believed a marriage license and murmured vows—often insincere and broken within days of their utterance—remedied the slightest hint of ruin.

"Blythe ...?" Uncertainty colored Brooke's voice. She released a hefty breath. "Mr. Burlington ...? Deuced awkward, this," she muttered beneath her breath. "What are your feelings regarding him?"

"I plopped a Grecian urn upon his conceited head last night. What's that tell you?" Twisting her mouth into a droll semblance of a smile, Blythe patted Brooke's shoulder. "Never fear. Any iota of girlish attraction I naively harbored for him vanished the instant he suggested I become his mistress."

Brooke's mouth hung slack. "He didn't."

Blythe raised a brow. "He did. After politely explaining why he couldn't marry a poor commoner."

Brooke cradled her stomach. "Oh, I'm quite furious, and that cannot be good for the babe. I hope you cracked his skull, the devious churl."

"I'm sure he's sporting a nasty, well-deserved headache." Blythe gathered a frilly pillow from the floor, and after tossing it onto the bed piled with several others, she rubbed an eyebrow. "And his heiress is welcome to him, although I feel sorry for the woman."

"As do I." Sighing, Brooke examined Blythe's gash. "How's your head today? Doctor Barclay said you weren't concussed, thank goodness."

"It's fine. Just a mite tender." Tristan meant to see this farce through, did he? A tiny part of her—truth to tell, a huge, soft, womanly chunk deep inside—thrilled that he'd defended her honor and risked censure by fabricating their betrothal. Still, he mustn't risk his life in an affair of honor.

Besides, not for an instant did she believe Phillips would fight fairly. If something happened to Tristan, she'd never be able to forgive herself. Surely gentlemen had a proviso for calling a duel off?

"How badly did I wound *him*?" Speaking Phillips's name was akin to gobbling fresh cow dung. She pressed two fingers to her temple where her head ached worse than she'd let on. The small cut, barely an inch long, was centered upon the walnut-sized, purplish lump near her temple.

"I'm not sure. Last night I didn't think his injury serious, though I may have misjudged." Straightening the pillows upon Blythe's four-poster bed, Brooke frowned then lifted a shoulder. "Lieutenant Drake paid him a call this morning to inquire who Mr. Phillips had named as his second. The Lieutenant met the physician leaving, and he claimed Mr. Phillips's wound was quite severe, that damage had been done internally. The gash has become putrid, and he battles a fever."

"I don't suppose the poker was altogether clean." God forgive her for the satisfaction that brought her.

"God willing, he'll die and the world will be spared his odious presence. And Lord Leventhorpe will be released from the duel." Brooke punched a lace-edged satin pillow. In anger or to fluff it? "I know that's horrid of me, but at this moment, I don't have a charitable thought in me."

"I might be responsible for his death then. I didn't intend to stab him." Blythe shuddered and tucked her chin to her chest. "But he deserved it, and yet I feel guilty. All I could think of was protecting myself. He meant to ravish me."

Brooke arranged the last pillow atop the cheerful green and turquoise counterpane before flying to embrace Blythe. "Stuff and nonsense. He is an evil man. Heath has told me of his reputation and that he's suspected of killing a ... a woman of ill-repute."

"My God. He is vile." Blythe may have done London and women a service if Phillips expired.

Tears glistened in Brooke's eyes, and she took Blythe's face between both hands. "You did what you had to. He isn't worthy of your sympathy. He meant to force you, and during a ball, at that. On your birthday. The man's daft as a Bedlam patient if he truly believed he'd succeed without severe consequences."

"Do you think he coerced Miss Sanford?" The iota of pity Blythe mustered was for gouty Lord Bexley. He'd seemed pleasant enough on the one occasion she'd met him, reeking of food and another other odd, medicinal odor.

"Perhaps, but she jumped at the opportunity to compromise you. A decent woman, frightened or not, would have promptly reported Phillips's suggestion. Remember, young women of quality are constantly chaperoned. Therefore, the likelihood of him carrying out his threat was minimal, as she knew that full well. I'm convinced that's why she helped him get you alone. I'd not waste your compassion on her."

"Miss Sanford spent a great deal of time with him unchaperoned. Perhaps her mother hoped to snare Phillips if Tristan avoided Miss Sanford's tentacles." Blythe pressed two fingers to her forehead. "Likely her mother's where she learned her despicable behavior."

A gentle rap upon the door preceded Brette's entrance.

"Yes, dearest?" Brooke clasped Blythe's hand.

"I've been sent to fetch you. The men grow restless. They're driving me near to shrieking with their pacing and babbling about the need for a special license in between making rather vile suggestions regarding Mr. Phillips. Each of which I agree with wholeheartedly." She raised her pert nose skyward. "I may have made a few fairly creative notions myself, one of which entailed him galloping Rotten Row atop a nail-laden saddle. Without pantaloons."

Blythe offered a wobbly smile and squared her shoulders. "Let's be about it then. From one blaze into another."

A few short minutes later, *too short*, she stood outside the study door. "Am I to speak with Lord Leventhorpe alone?"

Brooke grasped the handle. "I think that best, don't you?"

"Yes. This conversation will be awkward enough without an audience." She preceded Brooke into the comfortable study decorated in beige and sage green. Unlike the Wimpleton's darkly paneled room, Heath preferred an airier atmosphere. Yesterday, she'd trimmed the ladder ferns in their wicker stand placed before the simple linen window panels.

Freddy and the men rose at their entrance, and Heath indicated a striped armchair in verdant shades adjacent to Tristan's.

Blythe met Tristan's unreadable gaze for a fleeting moment as she made her way to the armchair, and her stomach flopped.

The planes of his face taut, he resumed his seat. Not precisely an exuberant groom.

"Do either of you require anything?" Brooke turned from the door, Heath at her side. She patted her hip. "Freddy. Come."

The corgi dutifully waddled to her, his tongue lolling and stubby tail wagging.

Given the empty brandy glass near Tristan, and the haggard lines bracketing his mouth and pleating the corners of his eyes, he could use a strong cup of coffee.

"I would dearly love a cup of my herbal tea. You know the mixture I use for soothing headaches? Would you mind terribly brewing a pot for me? The herbs are in a marked tin in the larder." Blythe managed a smile for Tristan. "Would you like coffee? We have a lovely Turkish blend."

"Yes. That would be most welcome." His reply wasn't exactly terse, yet neither was it warm. Grayishpurple half-moon shadows ringing his eyes attested to a sleep-deprived night.

"I shall give you fifteen minutes alone before I have the tea and coffee brought in." After giving Blythe an encouraging smile that didn't diminish the apprehension shining in Brooke's eyes, she swept from the room.

"I'll return within a half hour to discuss the settlement terms with you both." Heath delivered a genuinely warm smile. "I confess to being delighted that you are to marry, though, I would have bet high odds against anything of the sort when you first met."

He closed the door softly behind him, and for several interminable moments, the room remained silent.

What was Tristan thinking? Did he regret his impulsive gesture?

"You are well, Blythe?" The gentleness of his inquiry propelled her gaze to his. Compassion and something more intense emanated from his beautiful eyes.

"Yes. Other than a slight headache, I haven't suffered ill effects." Except a restless night and a reputation tainted beyond redemption. A room full of the *ton's* denizens had seen her partially clothed. It mattered not that Phillips hadn't been successful in despoiling her.

Tristan folded his hands in his lap then promptly unclasped them and laid his palms upon his black clad thighs. "You recall what happened, then?"

"If that's your way of asking if I remember agreeing that we are to be married, yes. I remember." Dragging in a great breath, Blythe jumped to her feet. She clasped her hands before her. "I feel I must tell you that I won't hold you to your offer. I know you said it to protect me in a perfectly ghastly situation."

Tristan stood as well, forcing her to crane her neck to meet his eyes. "Why were you in the library alone with him?"

"I ..." She spun away, not wanting to think about what had happened, how close she'd come to being ravished. Her knees grew shaky and her chest tightened with remembered fear as a shiver wracked her. She rubbed the raised flesh along her bare arms. "I was trying to find you."

"In the library? Why would you think to search for me there and not the ballroom or card room?"

The sunny rays filtering through the window enticed her, and she sought their tepid warmth. "I overheard Miss Sanford and her mother scheming last night and wanted to warn you of their intent to entrap you. When I entered the library, Phillips restrained me while Miss Sanford locked the door."

A robin swooped to the ground below the elder, and after giving her an inquisitive look, took to searching for insects.

"You meant to protect me? What did they plot?"

She nodded, shortly. "That you'd be found in a compromising situation with Miss Sanford at the ball and thus be forced to marry her."

He laughed, a warm, soothing rumble, filling the room and surprising her with his genuine amusement.

"You aren't angry?" She frowned, canting her head. "I should think you'd be furious."

With measured steps, he approached her, a mysterious bend to his mouth.

She dropped her gaze to the floor, afraid he'd see her love for him shining in her eyes.

"Ah, Fate had another plan, and Miss Sanford's duplicitous actions compelled me to claim you as mine." He cupped her shoulders, his large hands heavy, yet comforting. "Something I've yearned to do for weeks, though I doubted I would ever have the right."

Blythe jerked her head up and squinted. Had she mistaken his meaning? "What exactly are you saying?"

"I'm saying that I want to marry you and no other." Tristan drew her, unresisting, into his embrace. He chuckled again as she gaped, unblinking, at him. He ran his thumb along her lower lip and slanted his head at the window. "You had better close your mouth before yonder bird thinks to perch upon its lusciousness."

Her focus slid to his lips, and she pursed hers. Did she do that intentionally, to torment him?

"You've not given any indication you considered me anything other than a casual friend." Leaning into his arms, Blythe searched his face, emotions dancing across hers. "At one time, you couldn't abide me."

He firmed his embrace, edging closer until his thighs brushed her skirt, and he could feel her trembling legs. Resting his cheek against her unmarred temple, he whispered into the sweet fragrance of her hair, "You vexed the hellfire out of me, causing more intense feelings than I'd ever had for a woman. I didn't understand them for what they were."

Her expression softened, drawing him into the depths of her sapphire eyes, trapping him in their guileless, mysterious spheres. "You are the most complex man. After you kissed me, I believed you'd decided you weren't romantically inclined toward me."

"Utter gibberish." He kissed her hairline before feathering kisses down her cheek and the length of her jaw, lingering at the provocative corner of her mouth. "I never had to battle attraction so hard in my life."

Her sooty-tipped lashes fluttered closed, and she breathed out a sigh.

Needing no further invitation, he claimed her mouth, urging her lips apart with the tip of his tongue, delving into the sweetness of her mouth.

Blythe stood on her toes and entwined her arms about his neck. Catching onto the art of kissing with alacrity, she mimicked his actions. Their tongues jousted in a timeless melody of passion, until his groin swelled uncomfortably, and they both panted for breath.

Tristan drew away first.

Tupping his closest friend's ward in the study wasn't done. Well, not before exchanging vows, in any event. Afterward ... He eyed the armchair, and an unexpected, most unwelcome flash of discomfort assailed him. Did he tell Blythe of his childhood humiliation?

No. Not now.

After they consummated their marriage, and he'd

231

introduced her to the blissful aspects of physical joining, he might be ready to share the tale with her.

Or perhaps he never would.

That ugliness was in the past. She was his future.

Tucking her to him, he murmured into her hair. "I suppose I ought to go down upon a knee and propose formally, only I'm reluctant to release you."

Blythe chuckled against his chest, her slender arms encircling his waist. "I rather think a proposal while being held in your arms is much more satisfying and romantic."

"Blythe Culpepper, will you honor me by consenting to become my wife?" He kissed her ear, and she giggled.

"What?" She nudged his ribs. "No dramatic protestations of undying love or how I've made you the happiest man on earth?"

He drew away a fraction, drinking in her flushed features. "If that makes you happy and is what you want, I shall be delighted to do both."

"Oh. Pooh. I don't need pretty speeches. A man's actions show his affection and character much more clearly than mere words, and last night you risked everything to protect me." The look she gave him sent his pulse sprinting, and his manhood gave an eager twitch.

Whoa, boy. Patience.

"Am I to assume your answer is yes?" Tristan framed her jaw with his forefinger and thumb, caressing the silky flesh of her jaw. "I am ecstatic."

"Yes. I'll marry you." She shook her head, the silvery curls glinting halo-like in the sunlight. "I certainly never dreamed I'd be eagerly anticipating wedding the stern, rigid man I met at Esherton Green."

"Eagerly?" He waggled his eyebrows wickedly.

She gave him a coy wink. "Indeed. Most eagerly."

"Excellent. I've already purchased the special license. The ceremony will need to take place tomorrow. I know that's rushing things a jot—"

Her fair brows furrowed, and she stepped from his embrace, giving him a tight, closed-lipped smile. "I'd hoped for more time. I realize the scandal of last night prohibits a lengthy betrothal, but a week or two to prepare for a wedding—"

"I'm afraid that's impossible." He rubbed his nape. Blast, he hadn't wanted to discuss the duel on the fringes of what *was* possibly the happiest moment of his life. "The duel takes place the day after tomorrow, and we must wed first, because if I'm injured or killed—"

Blythe gasped, and balled her fists. "You mean to go through with the challenge? The day after we wed?"

He hadn't expected Blythe to be thrilled about the notion. Given the furious glint in her eye, she wouldn't concede easily. In fact, he hadn't intended to tell her about the duel until after the deed was done. That had seemed bloody brilliant when he'd first contemplated it. If Phillips bested him, she'd be married and widowed in under twenty-four hours, and she needed to know that Tristan had legally provided for her.

"You cannot meet that swine." Her chest rose and fell rapidly with her agitation. "He's a cur and a cheat. He'll not fight nobly, and you must know that to be true."

"It's a matter of my honor, Blythe." Mere moments ago, happiness and something akin to adoration had shone in her eyes. Betrayal shadowed her exquisite features now. He touched her arm. "A man is nothing if he does not keep his word. My honor is paramount to me."

Pursing her pretty mouth, she brushed a curl from her forehead. "According to Brooke, Phillips is gravely ill from the wound I inflicted. He won't be able to meet you. I'm surprised you didn't know that."

He did, yet didn't believe a word. Phillips was a bloody coward and would use any excuse to waylay the inevitable confrontation. In fact, at Tristan's behest, Drake and Whitehouse watched Phillips's residence, lest he try to sneak away. Again.

"I shall wait until he is recovered then. However, meet him I shall." Phillips couldn't be permitted to live and despoil more innocents. And if Miss Sanford had the right of it, he might be guilty of more appalling crimes. "He's escaped justice far too many times. He must be held accountable."

She closed her eyes, her lips trembling. Her lashes slowly lifted, and his heart turned to stone at the resignation and defeat in her eyes. "Then I regret, my lord, that I must decline your offer of marriage. I'll not be married and widowed within a day's time."

"Be sensible. Your reputation is in tatters. I offer you my name and security." He reached for her, and she fled behind the desk.

Shrugging, she placed the porcelain inkwell upon its matching tray. "I hadn't intended to marry well. I'll retire to the country."

"Blythe ..."

Three sharp raps echoed outside the door before it swung open. Lady Ravensdale, Raven, and a footman bearing a laden tray stood there smiling expectantly.

The moment they cleared the entrance, Blythe bolted for the exit.

"Blythe, wait, please." Tristan's long strides ate the distance across the leaf-patterned Axminster carpet.

Lady Ravensdale swung her confused gaze between them. "Is something amiss?"

Blythe reached her, and neck bent, shook her head. "No. I simply have no desire to be widowed the day after I marry. So, I've refused Lord Leventhorpe's offer of marriage."

"You have? Truly?" Ravensdale's confounded expression would have earned a chuckle and likely a taunt or two had the circumstances been different.

"Oh, Blythe." Lady Ravensdale crestfallen countenance revealed her devastation.

Without marriage, Blythe was utterly ruined.

"I'm sorry. Please forgive me. I know what this means." She offered a tremulous smile. "I shall pack at once.

Folly whispers marriage is a scheme for
contentment, but in truth, marriage is strenuous work.
~Dignity and Decorum—The Genteel Lady's
Guide to Practical Living

13

"There, that's the last of them. I feel quite wicked owning this much clothing." Early the next morning, Blythe placed the last of her unmentionables in her trunk.

Brooke promised to send the chest along later. For the journey home, Blythe would make do with a valise. Wisdom decreed she take a satchel in the event of unforeseen circumstances, although the trip to Culpepper Park could be achieved in a day.

The new house was habitable according to Brooke, though not fit for entertaining. That suited Blythe perfectly. Months might pass before she'd be in the mood for company.

Meg, Blythe's abigail since arriving in London,

agreed to journey with her, though Meg had no desire to remain in the countryside and would promptly return to London. No matter. Blythe had seen to her toilette for years. She didn't require a maid.

"Are you positive you won't reconsider?" Blaike sniffled into her handkerchief.

This separation would be the first for the sisters.

Blaire tortured her square scrap of cloth, twisting and tormenting its damp length repeatedly. "This whole affair is wretchedly unjust. I don't believe I care for London after all. Such supercilious people. Why, you are the victim. How dare they judge you?"

"You should at least stay at Heath's estate. There's no staff or furnishings at Culpepper Park." Brette passed Blythe a pair of slippers. "I'll allow, I'm quite miffed that you are to go alone."

Stay in a mausoleum of a manor—Heath's unflattering description—and with strangers for staff? Dreadful, by any measure. Returning to the dairy's familiar security and comfort held far more appeal.

"I understand, Brette, but we've discussed this already." A dozen times or more. "It's what I want, and besides, our old furniture was moved to the new house." Considerable effort went into her forced, cheerful smile. "I shall be fine."

"Hmph." A vulgar noise escaped Brette.

Blythe carefully tucked the embroidered slippers underneath a gown. She'd likely never wear either at Culpepper Park. The trunk overflowed with beautiful clothing and fallals, most unsuitable for a country gentlewoman. Heath insisted she take her new wardrobe, however.

"Why shouldn't everyone leave then?" Legs dangling over her chair's arm, Blaike gesticulated into the air.

"I'm the one unacceptable to Society. If I leave immediately, we hope to lessen the shadow cast over the rest of you. If everyone departs hastily, that implies you are guilty as well, and you are not. I won't have you disparaged on my account. For respectability's sake, I shall retain one or two servants from the village, so put that fear aside."

"I thought, perhaps, you weren't averse to Lord Leventhorpe. You'd spent a considerable amount of time in his company these past weeks, and that day at Gunter's, he looked like a man besotted." Blaike sent Blaire a silent message and threw her kerchief atop the night table.

Ah, the twins had noticed the tense exchange between Blythe and Tristan that day.

"He did indeed." Scarcely pausing, Blaike launched another protest. "Won't you reconsider?

Heath says his lordship is a dab hand at pistols. You should trust him."

Trust Heath or Tristan?

She did trust them both. Phillips, however, garnered the same confidence as Lucifer.

"Girls, I'm to depart within the hour. What's done is done. I've refused Lord Leventhorpe, and that is the end of it. He was most gallant to claim a false betrothal and offer to wed me to preserve my status. I do harbor a fanciful hope that since I cried off, he won't feel the need to follow through with that ridiculous duel." After all, he couldn't claim her as his affianced, and consequently the reason for his challenge no longer existed. Then again, men were so blasted difficult and prideful, he might pursue the idiocy.

Blythe had seen one way to offer Tristan a reprieve from the duel and save face as well as preserve his honor. If only he would put aside his confounded stubbornness and seize the opportunity.

God, please, let him.

If he didn't, she would pray Phillips wouldn't recover, and what manner of foulness did that make her? Wishing for a man's death?

A pout upon her lips, Brette wandered to the window. Parting the lace, she eyed the sky. "The weather has taken a sour turn. Perchance you should

240

delay your departure. Those clouds look as ugly as the ones that brought that fierce storm the day Heath arrived at Esherton Green."

"Looking like a bedraggled puppy." Blaire grinned for the first time today.

Blaike snickered. "A cross mutt too."

"He could have caught a nasty chill." Glancing behind her, Brette frowned, her worried gaze shifting from the full trunk to Blythe. "I wish you'd wait until this bluster passes. It makes me uneasy to have you traveling in foul weather."

"In England, a cloudy sky is hardly unusual, and neither are summer rains. The road is quite passable, even after a good shower. I'm not concerned." Bless Brette's heart, she simply sought a means to persuade Blythe to stay.

For the girls' sake, she couldn't. The sooner she put distance between herself and them, the better. *Le beau monde* considered her soiled goods, and much like a spoiled piece of fruit spread rot to others nearby, her presence tainted the rest of her family. Besides, she possessed no desire to endure the speculation regarding her pathetically short-lived betrothal.

Oddly, Burlington's treachery bothered her little. She was more peeved at herself for being a ninny and judging a man by his outward appearance. It chaffed to admit she'd been shallow as a puddle.

After she'd agreed to wed Tristan, crying off pierced like a double-edged blade—deep, and lethal. Her heart had nearly fragmented when she'd told Tristan she wouldn't marry him. But if it meant his life might be spared ... She shrugged mentally and offered a conciliatory smile to the distraught girls. "Sometimes we must make sacrifices so those we love won't suffer."

"Hmph." Flopping against her chair and kicking her feet in the air, Blaike shook her head. "And sometimes, those who love you don't give a cow's stinky behind what others think."

"I must go." London held no appeal for Blythe any longer, and the sooner she departed, the sooner she could nurse her mangled heart.

Six hours later, swathed in her sensible wool traveling cloak, Blythe warmed her gloved hands before a sooty stone fireplace in The Coach and Arms common room. Damp to her marrow, she flexed her jaw to still her chattering teeth. God's bones, she was half frozen. The sputtering fire valiantly sent a plume of orange sparks skyward, failing to thaw her stiff fingers and toes.

With its bare-beamed ceiling and darkish interior, the modest inn smelled of stale ale and fresh bread. More importantly, it provided a haven from the unremitting torrents.

London's earlier blanket of pewter clouds had transformed into a churning, black tempest complete with lashing rain, bursts of lightning, and deafening thunder. They'd barely traveled ten torturous miles the last three hours; the roads had become impossibly mucky and impassable. The tenacious driver and team had pressed onward as far as they could. With the wrathful charcoal sky showing no signs of easing its tantrum, and dusk flirting across the horizon, Blythe bid him stop at the next lodgings.

Since leaving London's outskirts, Meg had sighed and complained incessantly, and by the time the carriage squished and slid to a halt in the inn's muddy courtyard, Blythe couldn't wait to send the pampered maid to the kitchen to make tea and inquire about a hot meal.

Evidently, the weather had caught several other travelers unawares as well. Besides Blythe, a young couple, who appeared to be newlywed, a kind-faced cleric, a trio of motley soldiers, and a couple of burly, tartan-clad Scots occupied the humble taproom. A formidable matron attired in crackling black bombazine, and who loudly ordered her mousy companion about, had also been present when Blythe arrived.

Every chamber was taken, excluding a miniscule, fireplace-less attic room, more closet than bedchamber, with scarcely enough space for a narrow cot, an uneven nightstand, and rickety chair.

From the dust-covered cobwebs gracing two corners, spiders had been the lone inhabitants for a long while. Grateful for a bed, Blythe didn't quibble at the exorbitant price the flustered innkeeper demanded. She hadn't slept last night, and today, the pounding winds hammering the carriage, as well as Meg's grumbling mile after miserable mile, had prevented any rest in the carriage.

What else was Blythe to do?

Sleep near the hearth or in a corner of the common room as the soldiers and Scots intended, or curl onto the carriage seat as her driver had volunteered to do?

Her head, bum, and back ached, and tears threatened constantly. Better the inadequate cupboard where she could cry in privacy than a public room where her virtue might be jeopardized.

Turning her profile to the soldiers' intent scrutiny, Blythe prayed her chamber boasted a sturdy lock or a strong bolt. Propping the chair beneath the handle might provide added protection. She bent her lips a fraction. Knitting needles were stronger than the chair's spindly legs.

Meg had fussed about having to sleep upon a pallet in the kitchen. Blythe ignored her carping and pointedly didn't invite the servant to share her tiny room. After an eternity in the carriage with the peckish servant, Blythe's head ached nearly as fiercely as her heart, and she needed the quiet and solitude the chamber promised. Accustomed as she was to years of hardship and want, the humble room reminded her of her bedchamber at Esherton Green. Besides, a pallet for the maid wouldn't fit in the chamber.

The innkeeper's red-faced wife, carrying a tray laden with heavenly smelling soup, bread, and cheese, bustled past.

"Miss, ifn' ye mean to sup, ye'll have to eat in here. The private rooms be taken, and two hirelin's, blast their lazy, ungrateful hides, didn't come to work. I can't be waitin' on ye upstairs. Yer maid will have to see to yer needs." She jerked her chins in the kitchen's direction, sending her crepey neck jostling. "Pompous chit, that one."

"In here is perfectly fine." Eyeing the occupied tables, Blythe leisurely removed her gloves. Three had

245

chairs available, or she could take a seat upon the wooden bench below the filmy window, which rattled in protest every now and then from a gust of contentious wind.

Holding hands and murmuring softly, the couple sank onto the bench, their heads close together.

Blythe wouldn't—couldn't bear to—perch on the end of their bench and listen to their enamored chatter. To save Tristan's life, she'd relinquished her opportunity for love, but that didn't mean she couldn't yearn for the intimacy the couple shared.

Which table would it be then?

The cantankerous elderly dame? The scruffy soldiers? The fuddled Scots, already gulping their third pint since arriving? Or the pleasant-faced Man of God?

With a friendly nod, he waved her to his corner table, set slightly apart from the rest in a partial nook beside the fireplace. "Please, lass. I'd be pleased to have your company."

Giving him a grateful smile, she untied her bonnet as she sank onto a well-worn chair. "Thank you, Reverend ...?"

"Reverend Heaven." He chuckled softly, a merry twinkle in his warm gaze.

Disbelief must have shown in her eyes.

As if praying, he pressed his hands together.

"Honestly. The name's of Welsh origins."

Returning his easy smile, Blythe laid her gloves and rain-splattered bonnet atop the gouged and dented tabletop. "I imagine, given your profession, it's been the subject of many conversations."

"Indeed. Mrs. Heaven's first name causes a bigger stir." He leaned forward and winked. "It's Angel. Not Angela or Angelina. Just Angel. We named our sons Gabriel and Michael."

Blythe chuckled. "Brilliant. You've no daughter?"

"Alas, no." He pulled his earlobe while casually scrutinizing the other occupants. "But we considered Mary or Martha."

Meg tromped into the taproom, her mouth bent into a belligerent scowl. She crossly plopped Blythe's and Reverend Heaven's food atop the table, sloshing stew over the bowls' edges in her frustration. "I'm being made to help in the kitchen."

Blythe checked her sharp retort. "It's kind of you to lend a hand. They are short staffed, and the inn is full."

"I care not. I am not a scullery wench. I didn't agree to this." She flipped a hand scornfully at their food. "First thing in the morning, I'm returning to London. You cannot stop me."

Meg lifted her nose as haughtily as an Almack's

patroness and stamped past the soldiers.

How did she propose to do that? By post chase? Without funds?

Blythe would pay for her return to the city, but Meg would have to seek other employment. A servant with airs proved intolerable, and Brooke would be advised of Meg's unacceptable attitude.

One scarlet-clad chap tilted his chair onto two legs and grasped Meg's arm in passing. "Interested in some company, sweetheart?"

"No, you foul oaf." Meg pushed him over then, amidst the hoots and guffaws of his compatriots, stormed into the kitchen, declaring, "I'm never leaving London again."

"That one's carrying a cartload of bitterness." Reverend Heaven buttered a piece of bread.

"She's unaccustomed to discomfort." Lifting her spoon, Blythe sniffed the stew appreciatively. "Had I known, I wouldn't have asked her to accompany me."

He tilted his head, his keen gaze assessing and nodded sagely. "You, I would venture, are familiar with hardship. I see pain and suffering in your eyes, but you haven't become bitter."

Yet.

She didn't want to become a lonely, cynical harpy.

Battling the harsh sting of tears behind her eyelids,

Blythe lowered her gaze and took a bite of the savory stew rather than answer.

"I've been told I'm a good listener, Miss ...?"

Startled, she blinked away her tears, her watery gaze springing to his.

Compassion emanated from his kindly face. "And I'm sworn to confidence."

"Forgive me. I'm Blythe Culpepper, and I'm returning to my family home near Cheshire after an ... unpleasant sojourn in London."

The outer door flung open, and a gust of frigid, wet air billowed in. Blythe shivered, still not warmed. She'd likely sleep in her clothes and cloak given she'd only seen one quilt atop the thin mattress in her teeny closet of a room.

At first light, she'd be on her way. Now that home loomed near, eagerness overtook her. She'd sorely missed the country. If she had her way, she'd never venture to Town again.

"That fellow arrived upon a huge horse, just now. No luggage either." Reverend Heaven chewed his bread thoughtfully, his elbow resting atop the table. "Must be in a great hurry, or he was caught unawares. I don't envy him. He's soaked through. Must be utterly miserable. Do you mind if he joins us as well? Looks like he could use something hot in his belly and our table is nearest the fireplace."

Casting a disinterested glance over her shoulder, Blythe faltered, and her breath refused to leave her lungs.

A man, an immense man, stamped his booted feet and shook off his sodden greatcoat. Water sprayed in all directions and puddled at his feet. He pulled his hat from his head, revealing dark auburn hair.

Tristan.

A tiny gasp escaped her, and she dropped her spoon. It bounced off the table and onto the floor, clanging loudly each time the metal careened off a surface.

"Do take care, miss." The irritable ebony swathed tabby narrowed her eyes and clasped her chest above her ample bosom. "You startled me so, I may swoon. My heart is not strong. Miss Timmons, my vinaigrette at once."

Miss Timmons cast a pained glance ceilingward before dutifully rummaging in a traveling case and momentarily procuring an engraved silver vial.

"Please forgive my clumsiness." What was Tristan doing here? Blythe determinedly forced down the swell of anticipation seeing him caused.

There might've been a number of reasons he'd stopped at this inn. He didn't live far from Esherton

Green. Mayhap there'd been an urgent need for him to return to his estate, and the vile weather had forced him to stop here as it had her.

Or perhaps Phillips had died—her heart pitched, bum over head—and Tristan decided to quit London rather than face the *ton* as a jilted man. She'd discerned quite some time ago that he endured assemblies and routes. He didn't enjoy them.

"Do you know him?" Reverend Heaven's question caught her off guard.

How should she answer? Yes. She knew him, and leave it at that? Yes. We were betrothed for two wonderful minutes? Yes, he was a pompous, aggravating boor, and she adored him with her entire being, enough to save his life by refusing to wed him?

Intent upon retrieving her spoon and regaining her composure before answering, Blythe bent and had clasped the handle. A pair of muddy boots appeared beside the table.

Bother and blast. And ... and damnation!

Her scrutiny slowly traveled from his mud-caked toes, past his muscled calves tucked into the dirt-pelted Hessians, skimmed his narrow waist, and followed his torso's vee to his wide, russet-covered shoulders. His size never failed to impress her.

Or others.

Every person stared their way, and Miss Timmons's mouth hung slack in awe.

I know the feeling, dear.

He'd removed his greatcoat and must have deposited the garment and his hat and gloves with the innkeeper.

She almost smiled.

Likely he didn't recognize the preferential treatment he received. He took it for granted, as did most gentry and peers.

It didn't take a scholar to recognize a nobleman flush in the pockets. No doubt the fawning hostler offered Tristan a room too, at the expense of another unfortunate guest who would have to find other accommodations or sleep before the cinder-covered hearth.

"Miss Culpepper." Tristan inclined his head the merest bit before his attention swerved to Reverend Heaven, now standing. "Tristan, the Marquis of Leventhorpe, sir. Thank you for entertaining my betrothed until I could join her."

"Betrothed, you say?" The Reverend's brows vaulted to the top of his forehead as he shook Tristan's extended hand. "I'm Reverend Heaven, my lord."

Tristan's expression didn't alter a jot at the cleric's unusual name.

"Formerly betrothed." Blythe leveled Tristan with what she hoped was an impassive stare. "What are you doing here?"

After the men took their seats, Tristan gestured for the innkeeper then summoned a crooked smile. "I called at Ravensdale's and was told you'd left for Esherton. I followed."

"You followed." She snapped her fingers. "Just like that? Had you no care for the dismal weather or your health?"

"Just like that." He grinned mischievously. "I did think to borrow Raven's greatcoat."

Reverend Heaven chuckled, his keen gaze sparking with interest.

"Reverend, I might have need of your services." Tristan patted his pocket and winked. "I have a special license. I've rather muddled things, and I hope to put that to rights."

Impossible.

Blythe kicked him beneath the table. "We've had this discussion."

Wedding him meant he would face Phillips. She could never live with herself if Tristan lost his life defending her. Far better to be alone and desolate, and know he lived, than alone and desolate if he died. Yet, refusing the thing she most wanted took her absolute

253

resolve.

The innkeeper hurried to their table, bearing a frothy tankard. He placed the mug before Tristan and foam trailed down the pewter side. "My lord?"

"Miss Culpepper dropped her spoon. Please bring another when you serve my meal. Have you a private dining room available?"

Tristan passed the man a coin, earning a gap-toothed grin that rapidly transformed into a fretful frown. "No private dinin' room, Sir. I might be able to arrange for ye to use a chamber for a short spell. This weather has us overflowin'. I'll need a few minutes to work somethin' out."

"If we could have use of a chamber, for half an hour even, I would certainly show my appreciation." Another coin changed hands.

Blythe leaned back in her chair. "Do you do that often? Bribe your way to achieve what you want?"

"I prefer to call it compensation for extra effort. He's overworked, and from the looks of this place, he could use the coin." Tristan combed the room from end to end and gave a half jerk of his head "He'll not receive a groat more than he's earned from them, despite the hardship having this many patrons at once has caused."

"I believe you require privacy." Reverend Heaven

stood. "I shall be warming myself before the fire if you should need me. Please excuse me, Miss Culpepper, my lord."

He took his chair with him, preventing anyone else from sitting at their table. Clever man. In a moment, he sat before the now roaring fire, legs extended, hands crossed atop his rounded abdomen, and eyes shut. Resting or praying?

"I have a chamber. We can talk there with the door ajar. I'll allow you ten minutes." Blythe gathered her belongings. Despite his nonchalance, blue tinged Tristan's lips, and he'd shuddered more than once. Probably soaked to the skin, and without a warm bed to sleep in, he might catch lung fever.

"That's all the time I require." Tristan nodded and stood. "Let me tell the hostler to hold my meal."

A few minutes later, and slightly out of breath from climbing three flights, she entered her miniscule chamber and immediately set about lighting the candle atop the nightstand.

Tristan leaned against the doorjamb, his arms crossed, grinning like a baboon. "I've seen carriages and biscuit tins with bigger interiors."

"You jest, but I either accepted this room or slept below." Surprised by the room's pleasant temperature, she released her cloak's frogs, before shrugging its weight from her shoulders.

Tristan moved to assist her.

He hung the cloak over a wooden peg beside the rock chimney then tentatively skimmed the gray stones nested together. Leaning against their heat, he smiled in satisfaction. "This is why this chamber is warm." He patted the rocks behind him. "The heat from the fire below radiates off them."

"That's all well and good, and I'm grateful I won't freeze in my sleep." Casting a wary glance at the open door, Blythe sat upon the mattress, its meager depth harder than frozen ground. Wiggling her bum, she attempted to find a comfortable position. A night sleeping upon this mattress and she'd ache from toe to nose. "Why did you follow me? I gave you my answer yesterday."

"You did, and at first I had determined to accept your rejection, and allow you to disappear from my life. Though, I must tell you, I've experienced gut punches that hurt less." He crossed his ankles, closed his eyes, and pressed into the rocks. "This is rather splendid. I can finally feel my fingers again."

"Tristan. Will you please make your point?" Exhausted, she had no more reserves, and the tears she'd held at bay for the past twenty-four hours stung her eyes again. "You've used five of your minutes blathering about nonsensical rubbish."

He opened his gorgeous, black-lashed eyes, his gaze slicing straight to her soul.

"I love you."

A sob escaped her, and she pressed her fist to her mouth, struggling for control.

In an instant, he was beside her then pulling her into his strong embrace. He smelled of horse and rain and sandalwood, and she'd never inhaled anything sweeter.

"I know why you refused me." He kissed the top of her head while running his huge hands over her back and shoulders.

"You do?" The great slab of his chest muscle muffled her words. "Of course you do. I told you. It's because you insist upon dueling Phillips."

"Liar." He squeezed her ribs.

Prepared to give him a set down, she stiffened her spine. "I am not—"

Tristan settled his strong mouth atop hers, his hot, voracious kiss stifling her protest and launching it to the Earth's remotest corner. "You will let me speak my piece, or I shall silence you with a kiss each time you open your delicious mouth." He dropped another breath-hitching kiss on her lips. "Understand?"

She nodded, a half-smile bending her lips. "I

rather like your kisses—"

In a flash, she lay upon her back, his mouth and tongue searing her senses. The cot shuddered, groaning and squeaking, underneath his substantial weight. She wound her arms around his back. Hardly the actions of a woman refusing a suitor.

But he loved her.

"I suspected the real reason behind your rejection. When I spoke with Miss Brette today, she confirmed it." Using his forefinger, he traced her jaw, sending spirals of sensation skittering everywhere. "If we didn't marry, I wasn't honor bound to see the challenge through."

"Wait until I see her—"

By the time he finished kissing her again, Blythe seriously considered closing the door, stripping him naked, and having her way with him. Where had he learned to kiss like that? To render her incapable of coherent thought as tantalizing currents sluiced through her? Punishment via kisses that turned her bones to jelly wasn't disagreeable at all.

"Is it true? Is that why you won't marry me, Blythe? Did you recant your acceptance in order to nullify my reason for challenging Phillips?" The anguish in his azure gaze lacerated her resolve.

"Yes." A tear leaked from her eye, and then

another. She cupped his stubbly jaw. "I love you. I'd die if you were injured or killed meeting Phillips. I know men, especially peers, have a code you live by, and I know how important your honor is to you. I'd rather live in disgrace for the remainder of my days then risk harm coming to you."

"If you are willing to forego respectability, and face rejection, gossip, and scandal to spare me, then I am willing to live with the dishonor of repudiating my challenge." He kissed her nose. "I don't know whether Phillips will survive his festered wound, but if he does, I won't face him on the field of honor."

"Truly, Tristan?" She searched his eyes for a sign of regret and found none. "Some might call you a coward or ridicule you."

He elevated a brow. "I find honor without a cause is worthless. You are my cause. Naught else matters."

Some men might be given to flowery and romantic speeches. The sincerity of Tristan's simple heartfelt words surpassed them all.

Pressing a tender kiss against her lips, he whispered, "Will you marry me? Here? Tonight?"

Tristan waited, his breath suspended and constricting his lungs, for Blythe's answer.

Each mile he'd ridden, rain dripping into his collar and wind blasting his face with ice-cold pellets, he'd kept one goal at the forefront of his mind: to convince her that the greatest honor he would ever know would be to make her his marchioness and begin his life anew with her.

The wonder of her had crept into the recesses, the very core, of his being, and entrenched her spirit into his innermost places. Nothing that had ever come before, nothing he would face in the future, compared to the need to make her his life's partner.

He'd finally healed of his past humiliation, and though he'd never deem large gatherings his favorite pastime, the fear haunting him for almost two decades had vanished. She'd vanquished it.

Love had healed and restored him, a man filled with self-loathing.

Lips parted, plump and reddened from his kisses, Blythe peered into his soul. "I shall gladly marry you, but you need to know something about me, Tristan."

He propped his head upon his hand as he caressed the creamy column of her throat. Her breasts' perky tips taunted him below the bodice of her simple poplin traveling gown.

"And what is that?" He brushed her hair from her forehead, enjoying the excuse to touch her.

"I'm an ordinary woman of simple origins. Yes, I've endured poverty. I've also been blessed with a loving, supportive family." She entwined her fingers with his. "I haven't been scarred by tragedy, nor are there dark secrets in my past which torment or cause me angst. Perhaps couples who overcome great odds and conflict are grateful when they finally admit their love as we have, but, honestly I cannot regret the peaceful, quiet, normal life I've lived."

"Ahem. Perhaps we should commence with a ceremony?"

Tristan whipped his attention to the gaping doorway framing Reverend Heaven then chuckled as he levered off the bed. "Yes, Reverend. We'll meet you below in five minutes."

"Miss Culpepper? You are in agreement?" Reverend Heaven scratched his left eyebrow. "Are you of age?"

"I am, to both." She scooted to a sitting position. "I celebrated my first and twentieth birthday two days ago."

Reverend Heaven rubbed his hands together. "Well then, I'd say the Almighty has been working overtime arranging this storm. By-the-by, I insist you

261

take my chamber, and I shall occupy this one." His wink wasn't the least chaste or holy. "Mine has a bigger bed."

An hour later, after having been congratulated soundly by the hostler, his wife, and the inn's occupants, who'd assembled to witness the simple ceremony, and after finally eating, Tristan guided Blythe into the reverend's former chamber.

The bed was indeed bigger. By a good six inches.

"Are you nervous?" Normally a female family member explained what a bride could expect on her wedding night. "Do you have questions about tonight?"

Blythe's smile wasn't that of a timid virgin as she stood before a cracked oval mirror and unpinned her hair. "I was raised on a farm, Tristan. I know the ways of males and females."

"Yes, well, there are differences." He swept his hand down his front. "No fur or feathers."

"Or tail." Looking pointedly at his coat, she laughed, the deep, musical chuckle that he adored. "I believe we need to be naked to do the job properly."

"Have I married a vixen?" He made short work of divesting his clothing until only his pantaloons remained. She might have been familiar with farm animal anatomy, but the engorged penis of a highly aroused man might be a mite much. Particularly a man of his stature and build.

She stepped from her dress, a bold goddess, and draped the garment over the chamber's single chair. Her stays and stockings followed, and in a few tantalizing moments, she untied one shoulder ribbon of her chemise. No false blushes or pretense of demureness.

That was his Blythe.

"Let me." He brushed her hand away while kissing her collarbone.

She shuddered and sagged against him, her breath coming in short pants. "I've wondered what it would be like to have you possess me."

The fabric slipped to her waist as he cupped her breasts from behind and continued to nibble the sensitive flesh of her nape and neck. "You've imagined bedding me?"

"Uh hum. But I believed you loathed me." Her head fell forward, and she clasped his forearms as he slowly explored her abdomen. Then lower.

A sound, half-gasp, half-moan, escaped her open mouth, as she pressed her plump buttocks against his rigid length, demanding to be freed of its constraint.

He nipped her shoulder and gave her a little shove. "Lie down."

She complied, scampering underneath the coarse sheets, her curious gaze riveted to the bulge at his groin.

He unbuttoned the falls and tugged his pantaloons off.

She chuckled throatily when his member sprang free. "I'm quite looking forward to experiencing that."

He pounced upon her. "What, no maidenly shyness?"

"None whatsoever." She lifted her arms in invitation, a saucy smile teasing one corner of her mouth. "Now, husband, why don't you introduce me to passion?"

"With pleasure, my love."

Her eyes grew sultry. "Oh, I don't doubt it will be immensely pleasurable."

And it was. Both times.

Schemes and goals motivated by
love and honor are the most noble of all.
~*Dignity and Decorum—The Genteel Lady's
Guide to Practical Living*

Epilogue

Bristledale Court, Late August, 1822

"Look, darling." Sitting at a tea table centered upon the veranda, Blythe pointed to a pair of fawns. They followed their mottled mother from the woods bordering Bristledale Court's expansive greens where Blaire and Blaike strolled, arm in arm, beneath matching white lace parasols.

The day, vibrant with sunshine and a cloudless cerulean sky, promised a sweltering afternoon.

"This year, the fallow deer herd is greater than usual." Tristan folded his news sheet, and after setting it aside, extended his hand. "Walk with me, please. I have something I'd like to discuss with you."

Blythe patted her mouth with her serviette before taking his hand and collecting her parasol. "Of course."

"You are enjoying your sisters' visit?" Tristan led her off the covered promenade and into an elaborate parterre featuring topiaries, hedges, and a circular koi pond teeming with silvery and orange koi as well as pink water lilies.

"Very much. I essentially grew up with four sisters. I miss them, and I never thought to admit it, but I miss the chaos too." A subtle fragrance perfumed the air, and Blythe bent to sniff the heather-toned lavender. Nearly time to harvest it for linen sachets.

He nodded, a contemplative expression creasing his handsome face. "I know we decided against me applying for guardianship of the twins, since Ravensdale is wholly honorable and will do what is best for them. This past fortnight, having had an opportunity to become acquainted with Blaire and Blaike, I've come to a conclusion."

Blythe sloped her parasol against the sun. "A good one, I hope."

He chucked her chin. "Never fear. I quite like your sisters. And that's why I think they need an education beyond the schooling you've told me about."

Blythe stopped short. "Are you serious?

Gentlewomen don't attend higher education."

"Blythe, they are quite brilliant, and they've a hunger for knowledge I'm loath to leave unsated. I don't think I've ever encountered two keener female minds."

"Well, I don't know whether to be miffed or pleased. Are you implying I'm a dimwit?"

"Nothing of the sort. You simply aren't leaving my side. Ever."

Blythe followed the twins' progress as they occasionally pointed to a bird or plant. "They are unique, aren't they?"

"They are. Do you think they'd be receptive to the notion, or would they feel like we were trying to rid ourselves of them?" He shaded his eyes from the glaring sun and stared after the oyster-and-Pomona-green clad pair. "It's an opportunity few women have. On the other hand, I fear it may set them up for disappointment later in life by giving them a taste of freedom they may not want to relinquish for marriage."

"Hmm, I suppose it might. We'll never know unless we put the suggestion to them." She tucked her hand into his elbow, deliberately pressing her breast into his arm. "Besides, sometimes relinquishing one's freedom is quite divine."

His wicked chuckle sent a jolt of desire straight to

her woman's center. Tristan had introduced her to an extremely creative and most satisfying bed sport this morning, which had restricted her liberty for several delicious moments.

"Ho, Leventhorpe." Drake waved as he, Whitehouse, and Brette, accompanied by several others, including Francine and Maddox, stepped onto the veranda.

Tristan returned his greeting. "Ah, the rest of our houseguests finally stir."

"Not everyone rises with the roosters, darling." Blythe sent him a teasing smile. "I do rather prefer sunrise myself."

"I know why you favor mornings." Tristan swung her into his arms. "You like a rousing romp first thing, Lady Leventhorpe."

"Indeed, I do." She laid her head against his chest, and he rested his chin atop her head. "Did Lieutenant Drake's news of Phillips's partial recovery cause you regret or angst?"

"Not a wit. I spent far too long fretting about Society's opinion of me, and I am enjoying the liberation immensely." He kissed her crown, giving her a little squeeze. "I'm thoroughly delighted you rendered him incapable of performing as a man. Who knew an infection could cause such damage?"

"I can't bring myself to feel the slightest regret." Fingering the button of his jacket, Blythe pursed her lips. Phillips wouldn't be ruining anymore women, though the knowledge he'd not be punished for the viler acts he was suspected of rankled. "Surely the House of Lords has the power to hold him accountable."

"Not for despoiling a willing woman, and there's no proof of aught else." He patted her shoulder, lingering to caress the sensitive spot at the juncture of her neck that turned her knees to custard. "What think you of the other news Whitehouse divulged?

"You mean Miss Sanford ... er, Lady Bexley?" In truth, the crafty jealousy she'd meant for evil had worked for good, and Blythe owed her a debt of gratitude. Not that a formal thank you would be forthcoming. "I pity her. Widowed within weeks, and banished by the heir to the dower house with a pittance of an allowance. Once her mourning period is over, she'll be prowling about for a new husband, or cats don't meow."

"That's true, although I referred to the tattle regarding Burlington."

Cocking her head, she permitted herself an impish grin. "Mrs. Hemple is to be congratulated on her good fortune for escaping the parson's mousetrap. Wise

269

woman, having Mr. Burlington shadowed. Three indiscretions in as many weeks. Tsk, tsk. She's well rid of him."

"I quite agree. I'd like to break his perfect nose for suggesting you become his mistress." Turning them toward their waiting guests, Tristan used the opportunity to wrap his arm about her trim waist and cup her ribs. "You've filled out a bit since we married."

"Are you suggesting I'm running to fat?" Contriving a playful pout, she swatted his arm. "Fine way to speak to your wife when she's increasing."

"You mistake my meaning, darling." Casting a deliberate glance at her swollen breasts, he waggled his eyebrows and bent his sculpted lips, perfect for blood-heating kisses. "I simply worried for the babe's and your health. I'm not complaining in the least."

"Devilish knave." Her contented smile betrayed her joy.

"And that's exactly why you love me." He dropped a kiss onto her crown. "Happy, my love?"

Blythe tilted her chin, cupped his angular cheek. "Beyond my grandest schemes."

About the Author

USA Today Bestselling, award-winning author COLLETTE CAMERON® scribbles Scottish and Regency historicals featuring dashing rogues and scoundrels and the intrepid damsels who re-form them. Blessed with an overactive and witty muse that won't stop whispering new romantic romps in her ear, she's lived in Oregon her entire life, though she dreams of living in Scotland part-time. A self-confessed Cadbury chocoholic, you'll always find a dash of inspiration and a pinch of humor in her sweet-to-spicy timeless romances®.

Explore **Collette's worlds** at
www.collettecameron.com!

Join her **VIP Reader Club** and **FREE newsletter**.
Giggles guaranteed!

FREE BOOK: Join Collette's The Regency Rose®
VIP Reader Club to get updates on book releases,
cover reveals, contests and giveaways she reserves
exclusively for email and newsletter followers. Also,
any deals, sales, or special promotions are offered to
club members first. She will not share your name or
email, nor will she spam you.

http://bit.ly/TheRegencyRoseGift

Follow Collette on BookBub
https://www.bookbub.com/authors/collette-cameron

From the Desk of Collette Cameron

Dearest Reader,

Oh, I couldn't wait to write Blythe and Tristan's story!

From the moment they met at Esherton Green, their verbal bantering and sniping provided the perfect segue into their story.

Tristan's has a secret he wants kept hidden, and Blythe just wants the simplicity of her country life back.

Both these characters surprised me in the end.

I'm so thrilled you chose to read ***The Marquis and the Vixen*** and see Blythe and Tristan through to their hard won happily ever after!

Please consider telling other readers why you enjoyed this book by reviewing it. Not only do I truly want to hear your thoughts, reviews are crucial for an author to succeed. **Even if you only leave a line or two, I'd very much appreciate it.**

So, with that I'll leave you.

Here's wishing you many happy hours of reading,

more happily ever afters than you can possibly enjoy in a lifetime, and abundant blessings to you and your loved-ones.

Connect with Collette!
www.collettecameron.com

Follow her on:
Twitter @Collette_Author
Bookbub.com/authors/collette-cameron
Facebook.com/collettecameronauthor
Instagram.com/collettecameronauthor
Amazon.com/author/collettecameron.com/
Goodreads.com/collettecameron
Pinterest.com/colletteauthor/

The Earl and the Spinster

The Blue Rose Regency Romances:
The Culpepper Misses, Book One

*Would you sacrifice everything save your family?
Even your virtue?*

Caution: This book contains one stern lord with a dark secret he wants kept at all cost, a beautiful spinster smarter than the average man, an endearing, portly Welsh Corgi known to pee on gentlemen's boots, and a passel of well-meaning sisters and cousins who find themselves in one conundrum after the other.

Brooke Culpepper resigned herself to spinsterhood when she turned down the only marriage proposal she'd likely ever receive to care for her sister and cousins. After her father dies, a distant cousin inherits the estate, becoming their guardian, but he permits Brooke to act in his stead.

Heath, Earl of Ravensdale detests the countryside and is none too pleased to discover five young women call the dairy farm he won, and intends to sell, their home.

Desperate, pauper poor, and with nowhere to go, Brooke proposes a wager. Heath's stakes? The farm. Hers? Her virtue. The land holds no interest for Heath, but Brooke definitely does, and he accepts her challenge. Will they both live to regret their impulsiveness?

Buy the first book of The Blue Rose Regency Romances: The Culpepper Misses historical series for a romping, emotional, and romantic adventure you won't want to put down.

Enjoy the first chapter of

The Earl and the Spinster

The Blue Rose Regency Romances:
The Culpepper Misses, Book One

Even when most prudently considered,
and with the noblest of intentions, one who
wagers with chance oft finds oneself empty-handed.
*~Wisdom and Advice—The Genteel Lady's
Guide to Practical Living*

*Esherton Green,
Near Acton, Cheshire, England
Early April 1822*

*W*as I born under an evil star or cursed from my
first breath?

Brooke Culpepper suppressed the urge to shake her fist at the heavens and berate The Almighty aloud. The devil boasted better luck than she. My God, now two *more* cows struggled to regain their strength?

She slid Richard Mabry, Esherton Green's steward-turned-overseer, a worried glance from beneath her lashes as she chewed her lower lip and paced before the unsatisfactory fire in the study's hearth. The soothing aroma of wood smoke, combined with linseed oil, old leather, and the faintest trace of Papa's pipe tobacco, bathed the room. The scents reminded her of happier times but did little to calm her frayed nerves.

Sensible gray woolen skirts swishing about her ankles, she whirled to make the return trip across the once-bright green and gold Axminster carpet, now so threadbare, the oak floor peeked through in numerous places. Her scuffed half-boots fared little better, and she hid a wince when the scrap of leather she'd used to cover the hole in her left sole this morning slipped loose again.

From his comfortable spot in a worn and faded wingback chair, Freddy, her aged Welsh corgi, observed her progress with soulful brown eyes, his muzzle propped on stubby paws. Two ancient tabbies lay curled so tightly together on the cracked leather sofa that determining where one ended and the other began was difficult.

What was she to do? Brooke clamped her lip harder and winced.

Should she venture to the barn to see the cows herself?

What good would that do? She knew little of doctoring cattle and so left the animals' care in Mr. Mabry's capable hands. Her strength lay in the financial administration of the dairy farm and her ability to stretch a shilling as thin as gossamer.

She cast a glance at the bay window and, despite the fire, rubbed her arms against the chill creeping along her spine. A frenzied wind whipped the lilac branches and scraped the rain-splattered panes. The tempest threatening since dawn had finally unleashed its full fury, and the fierce winds battering the house gave the day a peculiar, eerie feeling—as if portending something ominous.

At least Mabry and the other hands had managed to get the cattle tucked away before the gale hit. The herd of fifty—no, sixty, counting the newborn calves—chewed their cud and weathered the storm inside the old, but sturdy, barns.

As she peered through the blurry pane, a shingle ripped loose from the farthest outbuilding—a retired stone dovecote. After the wind tossed the slat around for a few moments, the wood twirled to the ground, where it flipped end over end before wedging beneath a gangly shrub. Two more shingles hurled to the earth, this time from one of the barns.

Flimflam and goose-butt feathers.

Brooke tamped down a heavy sigh. Each structure on the estate, including the house, needed some sort of repair or replacement: roofs, shutters, stalls, floors, stairs, doors, siding...dozens of items required fixing, and she could seldom muster the funds to go about it properly.

"Another pair of cows struggling, you say, Mr. Mabry?"

Concern etched on his weathered features, Mabry wiped rain droplets from his face as water pooled at his muddy feet.

"Yes, Miss Brooke. The four calves born this mornin' fare well, but two of the cows, one a first-calf heifer, aren't standin' yet. And there's one weak from birthin' her calf yesterday." His troubled gaze strayed to the window. "Two more ladies are in labor. I best return to the barn. They seemed fine when I left, but I'd as soon be nearby."

Brooke nodded once. "Yes, we mustn't take any chances."

The herd had already been reduced to a minimum by disease and sales to make ends meet. She needed every shilling the cows' milk brought. Losing another, let alone two or three good breeders...

No, I won't think of it.

She stopped pacing and forced a cheerful smile. Nonetheless, from the skeptical look Mabry speedily masked, his thoughts ran parallel to hers—one reason she put her trust in the man. Honest and intelligent, he'd worked alongside her to restore the beleaguered herd and farm after Papa died. Their existence, their livelihood, everyone at Esherton's future depended on the estate flourishing once more.

"It's only been a few hours." *Almost nine, truth to tell.* Brooke scratched her temple. "Perhaps the ladies need a little more time to recover." *If they recovered.* "The calves are strong, aren't they?" *Please, God, they must be.* She held her breath, anticipating Mabry's response.

His countenance lightened and the merry sparkle returned to his eyes. "Aye, the mites are fine. Feedin' like they're hollow to their wee hooves."

Tension lessoned its ruthless grip, and hope peeked from beneath her vast mound of worries.

Six calves had been guaranteed in trade to her neighbor and fellow dairy farmer, Silas Huffington, for the grain and medicines he'd provided to see Esherton Green's herd through last winter. Brooke didn't have the means to pay him if the calves didn't survive—though the old reprobate had hinted he'd make her a deal of a much less respectable nature if she ran short of cattle with which to barter. Each pence she'd stashed away—groat by miserable groat, these past four years—lay in the hidden drawer of Papa's desk and must go to purchase a bull.

Wisdom had decreed replacing Old Buford two years ago but, short on funds, she'd waited until it was too late. His heart had stopped while he performed the duties expected of a breeding bull. Not the worst way to cock up one's toes...er, hooves, but she'd counted on him siring at least two-score calves this season and wagered everything on the calving this year and next. The poor brute had expired before he'd completed the job.

Her thoughts careened around inside her skull. Without a bull, she would lose everything.

My home, care of my sister and cousins, my reasons for existing.

She squared her shoulders, resolution strengthening her. She still retained the Culpepper sapphire parure set. If all else failed, she would pawn the jewelry. She'd planned on using the money from the gems' sale to bestow small marriage settlements on the girls. Still, pawning the set was a price worth paying to keep her family at Esherton Green, even if it meant that any chance of her sister and three cousins securing a decent match would evaporate faster than a dab of milk on a hot cook stove. Good standing and breeding meant little if one's fortune proved meaner than a churchyard beggar's.

"How's the big bull calf that came breech on Sunday?" Brooke tossed the question over her shoulder as she poked the fire and encouraged the blaze to burn hotter. After setting the tool aside, she faced the overseer.

"Greediest of the lot." Mabry laughed and slapped his thigh. "Quite the appetite he has, and friendly as our Freddy there. Likes his ears scratched too."

Brooke chuckled and ran her hand across Freddy's spine. The dog wiggled in excitement and stuck his rear legs straight out behind him, gazing at her in adoration. In his youth, he'd been an excellent cattle herder. Now he'd gone fat and arthritic, his sweet face gray to his eyebrows. On occasion, he still dashed after the cattle, the instinctive drive to herd deep in the marrow of his bones.

Another shudder shook her. Why was she so blasted cold today? She relented and placed a good-sized log atop the others. The feeble flames hissed and spat before greedily engulfing the new addition. Lord, she prayed she wasn't ailing. She simply couldn't afford to become ill.

A scratching at the door barely preceded the entrance of Duffen bearing a tea service. "Gotten to where a man cannot find a quiet corner to shut his eyes for a blink or two anymore."

Shuffling into the room, he yawned and revealed how few teeth remained in his mouth. One sock sagged around his ankle, his grizzled hair poked every which way, and his shirttail hung askew. Typical Duffen.

"Devil's day, it is." He scowled in the window's direction, his mouth pressed into a grim line. "Mark my words, trouble's afoot."

Not quite a butler, but certainly more than a simple retainer, the man, now hunched from age, had been a fixture at Esherton Green Brooke's entire life. He loved the place as much as, if not more than, she, and she couldn't afford to hire a servant to replace him. A light purse had forced Brooke to let the household staff go when Papa died. The cook, Mrs. Jennings, Duffen, and Flora, a maid-of-all-work, had stayed on. However, they received no salaries—only room and board.

The income from the dairy scarcely permitted

Brooke to retain a few milkmaids and stable hands, yet not once had she heard a whispered complaint from anyone.

Everybody, including Brooke, her sister, Brette, and their cousins—Blythe, and the twins, Blaike and Blaire—did their part to keep the farm operating at a profit. A meager profit, particularly as, for the past five years, Esherton Green's legal heir, Sheridan Gainsborough, had received half the proceeds. In return, he permitted Brooke and the girls to reside there. He'd also been appointed their guardian. But, from his silence and failure to visit the farm, he seemed perfectly content to let her carry on as provider and caretaker.

"Ridiculous law. Only the next male in line can inherit," she muttered.

Especially when he proved a disinterested bore. Papa had thought so too, but the choice hadn't been his to make. If only she could keep the funds she sent to Sheridan each quarter, Brooke could make something of Esherton and secure her sister and cousins' futures too.

If wishes were gold pieces, I'd be rich indeed.

Brooke sneezed then sneezed again. Dash it all. A cold?

The fresh log snapped loudly, and Brooke started.

The blaze's heat had failed to warm her opinion of her second cousin. She hadn't met him and lacked a personal notion of his character, but Papa had hinted that Sheridan was a scallywag and possessed unsavory habits.

A greedy sot, too.

The one time her quarterly remittance had been late, because Brooke had taken a tumble and broken her arm, he'd written a disagreeable letter demanding his money.

His money, indeed.

Sheridan had threatened to sell Esherton Green's acreage and turn her and the foursome onto the street if she ever delayed payment again.

A ruckus beyond the entrance announced the girls' arrival. Laughing and chatting, the blond quartet billowed into the room. Their gowns, several seasons out of fashion, in no way detracted from their charm, and pride swelled in Brooke's heart. Lovely, both in countenance and disposition, and the dears worked hard too.

"Duffen says we're to have tea in here today." Attired in a Pomona green gown too short for her tall frame, Blaike plopped on to the sofa. Her twin, Blaire, wearing a similar dress in dark rose and equally inadequate in length, flopped beside her.

Each girl scooped a drowsy cat into her lap. The cats' wiry whiskers twitched, and they blinked their sleepy amber eyes a few times before closing them once more as the low rumble of contented purrs filled the room.

"Yes, I didn't think we needed to light a fire in the drawing room when this one will suffice." As things stood, too little coal and seasoned firewood remained to see them comfortably until summer.

Brette sailed across the study, her slate-blue gingham dress the only one of the quartet's fashionably long enough. Repeated laundering had turned the garment a peculiar greenish color, much like tarnished copper. She looped her arm through Brooke's.

"Look, dearest." Brette pointed to the tray. "I splurged and made a half-batch of shortbread biscuits. It's been so long since we've indulged, and today is your birthday. To celebrate, I insisted on fresh tea leaves as well."

Brooke would have preferred to ignore the day.

Three and twenty.

On the shelf. Past her prime. Long in the tooth. Spinster. *Old maid.*

She'd relinquished her one chance at love. In order to nurse her ailing father and assume the care of her young sister and three orphaned cousins, she'd refused Humphrey Benbridge's proposal. She couldn't have put her happiness before their welfare and deserted them when they needed her most. Who would've cared for them if she hadn't?

No one.

Mr. Benbridge controlled the purse strings, and Humphrey had neither offered nor been in a position to take on their care. Devastated, or so he'd claimed, he'd departed to the continent five years ago.

She'd not seen him since.

Nonetheless, his sister, Josephina, remained a friend and occasionally remarked on Humphrey's travels abroad. Burying the pieces of her broken heart beneath hard work and devotion to her family, Brooke had rolled up her sleeves and plunged into her forced role as breadwinner, determined that sacrificing her love not be in vain.

Yes, it grieved her that she wouldn't experience a man's passion or bear children, but to wallow in doldrums was a waste of energy and emotion. Instead, she focused on building a future for her sister and cousins—so they might have what she never would—and allowed her dreams to fade into obscurity.

"Happy birthday." Brette squeezed her hand.

Brooke offered her sister a rueful half-smile. "Ah,

I'd hoped you'd forgotten."

"Don't be silly, Brooke. We couldn't forget your special day." Twenty-year-old Blythe—standing with her hands behind her—grinned and pulled a small, neatly-wrapped gift tied with a cheerful yellow ribbon from behind her. Sweet dear. She'd used the trimming from her gown to adorn the package.

"Hmph. Need seedcake an' champagne to celebrate a birthday properly." The contents of the tray rattled and clanked when Duffen scuffed his way to the table between the sofa and chairs. After depositing the tea service, he lifted a letter from the surface. Tea dripped from one stained corner. "This arrived for you yesterday, Miss Brooke. I forgot where I'd put it until just now."

If I can read it with the ink running to London and back.

He shook the letter, oblivious to the tawny droplets spraying every which way.

Mabry raised a bushy gray eyebrow, and the twins hid giggles by concealing their faces in the cat's striped coats.

Brette set about pouring the tea, although her lips twitched suspiciously.

Freddy sat on his haunches and barked, his button eyes fixed on the paper, evidently mistaking it for a tasty morsel he would've liked to sample. He licked his chops, a testament to his waning eyesight.

"Thank you, Duffen." Brooke took the letter by one soggy corner. Holding it gingerly, she flipped it over. No return address.

"Aren't you going to read it?" Blythe set the gift on the table before settling on the sofa and smoothing her skirt. They didn't get a whole lot of post at Esherton. Truth be known, this was the first letter in months. Blythe's gaze roved to the other girls and the equally eager expressions on their faces. "We're on pins and needles," she quipped, fluttering her hands and winking.

Brooke smiled and cracked the brownish wax seal with her fingernail. Their lives had become rather monotonous, so much so that a simple, *soggy*, correspondence sent the girls into a dither of anticipation.

My Dearest Cousin...

Brooke glanced up. "It's from Sheridan.

The Lord and the Wallflower

The Blue Rose Regency Romances:
The Culpepper Misses, Book Three

How many times should a man propose before finally giving up?

Caution: This book contains a rector too sexy for his own good, a match-making, meddling miss who finds herself in one conundrum after another, an endearing portly Welsh Corgi, and a troupe of well-meaning, interfering cousins and sisters

He thought his adventures were over.

A rogue reluctantly turned rector, Alexander Hawksworth, prefers soirées to sermons and parties to prayers. Though impoverished, he seizes every opportunity to escape parish duties, preferring to hob nob with London's finest–especially after the precocious and petite Brette Culpepper arrives in Town. When he unexpectedly inherits an earldom, he's determined to make her his countess. Until he's accused of murdering the previous earl.

Then she burst headlong into his life.
New to Society, Brette adores the whirlwind social scene, the stream of invitations, the slightly-sensual verbal sparring with the devilishly attractive, much too witty, and oh, so unsuitable Mr. Hawksworth. But her fairytale existence crashes to a halt when rumors circulate she's a peer's illegitimate granddaughter, and a newly appointed guardian emerges, intent on forcing her to wed an elderly degenerate.

Time is against them as Alex struggles to clear his name and deliver the woman he loves from an unthinkable fate.

Buy the third book in The Blue Rose Regency Romances: The Culpepper Misses historical series for a romping, emotional, and romantic adventure you won't want to put down.

A Kiss for a Rogue

The Honorable Rogues™, Book One

Formerly titled A Kiss for Miss Kingsley

A lonely wallflower. A future viscount. A second chance at love.

Olivia Kingsley didn't expect to be swept off her feet and receive a marriage proposal two weeks into her first Season. However, one delicious dance with Allen Wimpleton, and her future is sealed. Or so she thinks until her eccentric father suddenly announces he's moving the family to the Caribbean for a year.

Terrified of losing Olivia, Allen begs her to elope, but she refuses. Distraught at her leaving, and unaware of her father's ill-health, Allen doubts her love and foolishly demands she choose—him or her father.

Heartbroken at his callousness, Olivia turns her back on their love. The year becomes three, enough time for her broken heart to heal, and after her father dies, she returns to England.

Coming face to face with Allen at a ball, she realizes she never purged him from her heart.

But can they overcome their pasts and old wounds to trust love again? Or has Allen found another in her absence?

This second chance Regency historical by a *USA Today* bestselling author will make you want to box Allen's ears and promise Olivia that **she will** find true love.

If you enjoy reading reunited lovers stories sprinkled with a dab of humor, suspense, and heart-warming emotion, then you'll adore Collette Cameron's tantalizing THE HONORABLE ROGUES SERIES™. Buy A KISS FOR A ROGUE and settle into your favorite reading nook for a rousing romantic adventure you can't put down.

Though this book can easily be read as a stand-alone, most readers prefer to read the series in order.

Enjoy the first chapter of

A Kiss for a Rogue

The Honorable Rogues™, Book One

A lady must never forget
her manners nor lose her composure.
~A Lady's Guide to Proper Comportment

London, England
Late May, 1818

"This is a monumental mistake."

God's toenails. What were you thinking, Olivia Kingsley, agreeing to Auntie Muriel's addlepated scheme?

Why had she ever agreed to this farce?

Fingering the heavy ruby pendant hanging at the hollow of her neck, Olivia peeked out the window as the conveyance rounded the corner onto Berkeley Square. Good God. Carriage upon carriage, like great shiny beetles, lined the street beside an ostentatious manor. Her heart skipped a long beat, and she ducked out of sight.

Braving another glance from the window's corner, her stomach pitched worse than a ship amid a hurricane. The full moon's milky light, along with the mansion's rows of glowing diamond-shaped panes, illuminated the street. Dignified guests in their evening finery swarmed before the grand entrance and on the granite stairs as they waited their turn to enter Viscount and Viscountess Wimpleton's home.

The manor had acquired a new coat of paint since she had seen it last. She didn't care for the pale lead shade, preferring the previous color, a pleasant, welcoming bronze green. Why anyone living in Town would choose to wrap their home in such a chilly color was beyond her. With its enshrouding fog and perpetually overcast skies, London boasted every shade of gray already.

Three years in the tropics, surrounded by vibrant flowers, pristine powdery beaches, a turquoise sea, and balmy temperatures had rather spoiled her against London's grime and stench. How long before she grew accustomed to the dank again? The gloom? The smell?

Never.

Shivering, Olivia pulled her silk wrap snugger. Though late May, she'd been nigh on to freezing since the ship docked last week.

A few curious guests turned to peer in their carriage's direction. A lady swathed in gold silk and dripping diamonds, spoke into her companion's ear and pointed at the gleaming carriage. Did she suspect someone other than Aunt Muriel sat behind the distinctive Daventry crest?

Trepidation dried Olivia's mouth and tightened her chest. Would many of the *ton* remember her?

Stupid question, that. Of course she would be remembered.

Much like ivy—its vines clinging tenaciously to a tree—or a barnacle cemented to a rock, one couldn't easily be pried from the upper ten thousand's memory. But, more on point, would anyone recall her fascination with Allen Wimpleton?

Inevitably.

Coldness didn't cause the new shudder rippling from her shoulder to her waist.

Yes. Attending the ball was a featherbrained

solicitation for disaster. No good could come of it. Flattening against the sky-blue and gold-trimmed velvet squab in the corner of her aunt's coach, Olivia vehemently shook her head.

"I cannot do it. I thought I could, but I positively cannot."

A curl came loose, plopping onto her forehead.

Bother.

The dratted, rebellious nuisance that passed for her hair escaped its confines more often than not. She shoved the annoying tendril beneath a pin, having no doubt the tress would work its way free again before evenings end. Patting the circlet of rubies adorning her hair, she assured herself the band remained secure. The treasure had belonged to Aunt Muriel's mother, a Prussian princess, and no harm must come to it.

Olivia's pulse beat an irregular staccato as she searched for a plausible excuse for refusing to attend the ball after all. She wouldn't lie outright, which ruled out her initial impulse to claim a *megrim*.

"I ... we—" She wiggled her white-gloved fingers at her brother, lounging on the opposite seat. "Were not invited."

Contented as their fat cat, Socrates, after lapping a saucer of fresh cream, Bradford settled his laughing gaze on her. "Yes, we mustn't do anything untoward."

Terribly vulgar, that. Arriving at a *haut ton* function, no invitation in hand. She and Bradford mightn't make it past the vigilant majordomo, and then what were they to do? Scuttle away like unwanted pests? Mortifying and prime tinder for the gossips.

"Whatever will people *think*?" Bradford thrived on upending Society. If permitted, he would dance naked as a robin just to see the reactions. He cocked a cinder-black brow, his gray-blue eyes holding a challenge.

Toad.

Olivia yearned to tell him to stop giving her that loftier look. Instead, she bit her tongue to keep from sticking it out at him like she had as a child. Irrationality warred with reason, until her common sense finally prevailed. "I wouldn't want to impose, is all I meant."

"Nonsense, darling. It's perfectly acceptable for you and Bradford to accompany me." The seat creaked as Aunt Muriel, the Duchess of Daventry, bent forward to scrutinize the crowd. She patted Olivia's knee. "Lady Wimpleton is one of my dearest friends. Why, we had our come-out together, and I'm positive had she known that you and Bradford had recently returned to England, she would have extended an invitation herself."

Olivia pursed her lips.

Not if she knew the volatile way her son and I parted company, she wouldn't have.

A powerful peeress, few risked offending Aunt Muriel, and she knew it well. She could haul a haberdasher or a milkmaid to the ball and everyone would paste artificial smiles on their faces and bid the duo a pleasant welcome. Reversely, if someone earned her scorn, they had best pack-up and leave London permanently before doors began slamming in their faces. Her influence rivaled that of the Almack's patronesses.

Bradford shifted, presenting Olivia with his striking profile as he, too, took in the hubbub before the manor. "You will never be at peace—never be able to move on—unless you do this."

That morsel of knowledge hadn't escaped her, which was why she had agreed to the scheme to begin with. Nevertheless, that didn't make seeing Allen Wimpleton again any less nerve-wracking.

"You must go in, Livy," Bradford urged, his countenance now entirely brotherly concern.

She stopped plucking at her mantle and frowned. "Please don't call me that, Brady."

Once, a lifetime ago, Allen had affectionately called her Livy—until she had refused to succumb to his begging and run away to Scotland. Regret momentarily altered her heart rhythm.

Bradford hunched one of his broad shoulders and scratched his eyebrow. "What harm can come of it? We'll only stay as long as you like, and I promise, I shall remain by your side the entire time."

Their aunt's unladylike snort echoed throughout the carriage.

"And the moon only shines in the summer." Her voice dry as desert sand, and skepticism peaking her eyebrows high on her forehead, Aunt Muriel fussed with her gloves. "Nephew, I have never known you to forsake an opportunity to become, er ..."

She slid Olivia a guarded glance. "Shall we say, become better acquainted with the ladies? This Season, there are several tempting beauties and a particularly large assortment of amiable young widows eager for a *distraction*."

Did Aunt Muriel truly believe Olivia don't know about Bradford's reputation with females? She was neither blind nor ignorant.

He turned and flashed their aunt one of his dazzling smiles, his deeply tanned face making it all the more brighter. "All pale in comparison to you two lovelies, no doubt."

Olivia made an impolite noise and, shaking her head, aimed her eyes heavenward in disbelief.

Doing it much too brown. Again.

Bradford was too charming by far—one reason the fairer sex were drawn to him like ants to molasses. She'd been just as doe-eyed and vulnerable when it came to Allen.

"Tish tosh, young scamp. Your compliments are wasted on me." Still, Aunt Muriel slanted her head, a pleased smile hovered on her lightly-painted mouth and pleating the corners of her eyes. "Besides, if you attach yourself to your sister, she won't have an opportunity to find herself alone with young Wimpleton."

Olivia managed to keep her jaw from unhinging as she gaped at her aunt. She snapped her slack mouth shut with an audible click. "Shouldn't you be cautioning me *not* to be alone with a gentleman?"

Aunt Muriel chuckled and patted Olivia's knee again. "That rather defeats the purpose in coming tonight then, doesn't it, dear?" Giving a naughty wink, she nudged Olivia. "I do hope Wimpleton kisses you. He's such a handsome young man. Quite the Corinthian too."

A hearty guffaw escaped Bradford, and he slapped his knee. "Aunt Muriel, I refuse to marry until I find a female as colorful as you. Life would never be dull."

"I should say not. Daventry and I had quite the

adventurous life. It's in my blood, you know, and yours too, I suspect. Papa rode his stallion right into a church and actually snatched Mama onto his lap moments before she was forced to marry an abusive lecher. The scandal, they say, was utterly delicious." The duchess sniffed, a put-upon expression on her lined face. "Dull indeed. *Hmph*. Never. Why, I may have to be vexed with you the entire evening for even hinting such a preposterous thing."

"Grandpapa abducted Grandmamma? In church, no less?" Bradford dissolved into another round of hearty laughter, something he did often as evidenced by the lines near his eyes.

Unable to utter a single sensible rebuttal, Olivia swung her gaze between them. Her aunt and brother beamed, rather like two naughty imps, not at all abashed at having been caught with their mouth's full of stolen sweetmeats from the kitchen.

She wrinkled her nose and gave a dismissive flick of her wrist. "Bah. You two are completely hopeless where decorum is concerned."

"Don't mistake decorum for stodginess or pomposity, my dear." Her aunt gave a sage nod. "Neither permits a mite of fun and both make one a cantankerous boor."

Bradford snickered again, his hair, slightly too

long for London, brushing his collar. "By God, if only there were more women like you."

Olivia itched to box his ears. Did he take nothing seriously?

No. Not since Philomena had died.

Olivia edged near the window once more and worried the flesh of her lower lip. Carriages continued to line up, two or three abreast. Had the entire *beau monde* turned out for the grand affair?

Botheration. Why must the Wimpletons be so well-received?

She caught site of her tense face reflected in the glass, and hastily turned away.

"And, Aunt Muriel, you're absolutely positive that Allen—that is, Mr. Wimpleton—remains unattached?"

Fiddling with her shawl's silk fringes, Olivia attempted a calming breath. No force on heaven or earth could compel her to enter the manor if Allen were betrothed or married to another. Her fragile heart, though finally mended after three years of painful healing, could bear no more anguish or regret.

If he were pledged to another, she would simply take the carriage back to Aunt Muriel's, pack her belongings, and make for Bromham Hall, Bradford's newly inherited country estate. Olivia would make a fine spinster; perhaps even take on the task of housekeeper in order to be of some use to her brother. She would never set foot in Town again.

She dashed her aunt an impatient, sidelong peek. Why didn't Aunt Muriel answer the question?

Head to the side and eyes brimming with compassion, Aunt Muriel regarded her.

"You're certain he's not courting anyone?" Olivia pressed for the truth. "There's no one he has paid marked attention to? You must tell me, mustn't fear for my sensibilities or that I'll make a scene."

She didn't make scenes.

The *A Lady's Guide to Proper Comportment* was most emphatic in that regard.

Only the most vulgar and lowly bred indulge in histrionics or emotional displays.

Aunt Muriel shook her turbaned head firmly. The bold ostrich feather topping the hair covering jolted violently, and her diamond and emerald cushion-shaped earrings swung with the force of her movement. She adjusted her gaudily-colored shawl.

"No. No one. Not from the lack of enthusiastic mamas, and an audacious papa or two, shoving their simpering daughters beneath his nose, I can tell you. Wimpleton's considered a brilliant catch, quite dashing, and a top-sawyer, to boot." She winked wickedly again. "Why, if I were only a score of years younger ..."

"Yes? What *would* you do, Aunt Muriel?" Rubbing his jaw, Bradford grinned.

Olivia flung him a flinty-eyed glare. "Hush. Do not encourage her."

Worse than children, the two of them.

Lips pursed, Aunt Muriel ceased fussing with her skewed pendant and tapped her fingers upon her plump thigh. "I would wager a year's worth of my favorite pastries that fast Rossington chit has set her cap for him, though. Has her feline claws dug in deep, too, I fear."

CPSIA information can be obtained
at www.ICGtesting.com
Printed in the USA
BVHW041814150920
588871BV00014B/806